T0078408

WHY "DIDN'T" I GET MARRIED?

EITHER BOAZ OR "NO-AZ," I'M WAITING ON "PURPOSE"

KAREN D. REID, Ph.D.

authorHOUSE®

AuthorHouse™
1663 Liberty Drive
Bloomington, IN 47403
www.authorhouse.com
Phone: 833-262-8899

Published by AuthorHouse 04/05/2021

ISBN: 978-1-6655-1308-1 (sc)
ISBN: 978-1-6655-1307-4 (e)

Library of Congress Control Number: 2021900625

Print information available on the last page.

CONTENTS

DEDICATION

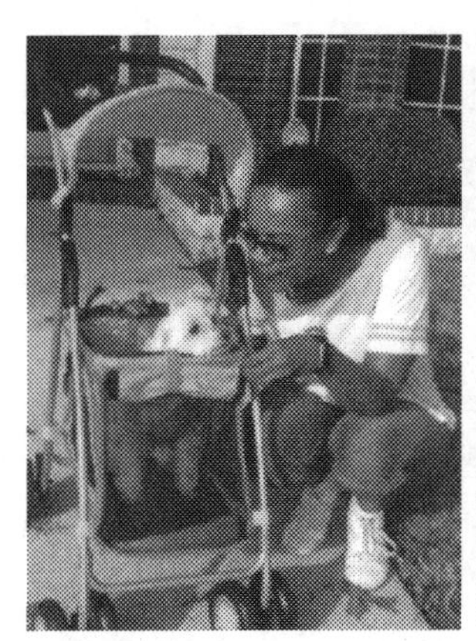

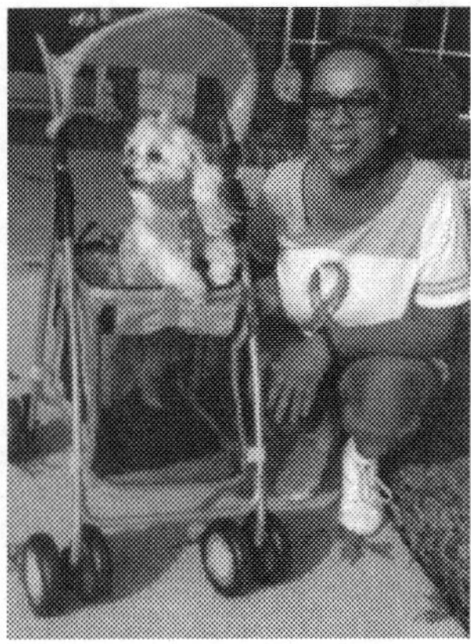

As of November 3, 2018, my "therapy dog," "Baby," is no longer with us. Despite my extreme phobia of dogs that I had most of my life, I literally lost the love of my life. If God had allowed "Baby" to recover, I would have written a book, entitled, The Miracle "Baby." I was desperately pulling for her because she had become the baby I never had, as she fulfilled a void like no one would understand. Because love conquers all things, her approval and affection is what helped me to overcome my fear of small dogs (only). I know that most people would say: "it was JUST a dog; get over it!" Well, that would be easy to say if you never had a dog, or you have family and/ or church members, or lots of friends to love you back.

When my nieces and nephews became too old to be my babies, and too busy to return my calls and texts, "Baby" absolutely did it for me. Her big, brown eyes staring me in the face always gave me something to look forward to. Following me to the bathroom and waiting for me to come out would warm my heart like you cannot imagine. In fact, I uninvited myself from a week-long, complimentary cruise with my family, in order to travel to their Dallas home to keep "Baby" from being boarded. Consequently, the other dog came with the agreement, but I managed to manage.

Not even realizing that Baby would be gone the following year, it was my paternal instincts that kicked in to make me step up. During that week, I hated to leave her alone while I went out to run errands. Sadly, I would leave her at the door looking up at me (not knowing that it would be our last week together). Then I would rush back to meet her, exactly where I left her. Now I totally understand the adage: "A dog is man's best friend."

To say the least, Baby taught me what it feels like to have that mother's intuition. Long before it was discovered, I kept telling my sister that something was wrong. She would always say: "Girl, there's nothing wrong with Baby; she just likes your attention. I had noticed that every time she needed to go upstairs, she would walk around in circles, as though she wasn't sure if she could make it. So when she finally made it to the top step, I would always celebrate her with my happy dance and a treat. She anticipated it, and would always dance with me. This would make my day and bring me so much joy.

She was a fighter too, just like her best buddy. Even with 4th-stage cancer, she took her pain gracefully and without whining or whimpering. And, as she hobbled around with an abscess as large as a lemon, she managed to continue climbing steps to be around the family. After a previous surgery and three veterinarians' opinions, she's better off now. Even so, life, holidays, and visits with the Blanches will never be the same without "Baby." I certainly empathize with my family who took great care of her for 12 years, an even bigger loss for them. I just wish that I could have spent time with her, just one last time before she was put to rest. "Death doesn't hurt, but life does." R.I.P. my sweet-little "Baby" girl.

PUBLICIST'S REVIEWS

By Ed Harris Sr., M.A.
Principle Consultant/Coach
The Sapient Alliance LLC
email: www. thesapientalliance@gmail.com

I am pretty intrigued and impressed by your ability to use vernacular to express yourself and to capture the attention of your reader. I was pretty amused by your stringing together of words to keep it 100. It made it a palatable, relatable document as opposed to being an academic document. The way you shared your personal journey gives an insight into situations that exist, and in many instances, taboo situations that are not often addressed. You actually put some brothers on notice, by informing them that just because you are a fine, attractive female, you are not waiting on anyone to do anything that you can do for yourself. Basically, you made it clear what you are interested in, what you look to avoid, and what you're hoping to instill as it relates to the interconnection and compatibility of individuals.

When you write about not being bamboozled or pulled into a relationship based on the premise of faulty engagement, it will make a person sit up in their seat, if they really take the time to read it. I loved the way you used the zingers, and I think that they are actually necessary because they keep it REAL. Some of the metaphoric conversation that you have is cutting edge, especially when you deal with the sensitivity of traditionalism, even as some folks do not honor the fact that it exists. Yet, you are pretty clear on the need for such things to be abolished.

Speaking to the experience with your biological father actually speaks to challenges that people face daily, especially from the generation that precedes us. People being committed to the vows and what ended up being acceptable, just by virtue of the times, still has a major impact today. Your articulation of the trickle-down effect caused me to "rock back on my heels."

In one section, you spoke directly to those who would condemn you. The church mothers may be appalled, but I love the statement that was made for those expecting you to say it a certain way. In essence you said: "This is not your typical conversation because I have to speak to you from the depths of my soul. Let me not mess you up, but I will not let you define me based on your jaded perspective. It's not that I'm trying to cut your legs from under you, but I need to make sure you understand that these practices that you are accustomed to, don't work for me."

And then you spoke out of your brokenness. There was authenticity in your pain; yet, the way you employed your pain does not appear to be a paralyzing tool in the book. In fact, it seems that your pain empowered you to find a voice that would not have been heard. Off the page, if people do not possess imagination, they cannot go where the author is. That's why your little zingers caused me to sit up and say, "No she didn't!" I could see you rolling your neck, with your hands on your hips, and saying, "don't get it twisted!"

I think you know that there are individuals who are going to read into this and be rubbed the wrong way. My concern in those areas is that it does not come at the expense of causing you additional, undue hardship. But when you take the risk of being candid and truthful, that happens; however, I think that you manage it well.

There are many different genres and avenues whereas this book can help people across the board. I think the potential is great, and I perceive it as even being a cutting edge, seminary tool. It sends messages to clergy and leaders that the manipulation of vulnerability is a sin. It's not necessarily the "Me Too Movement," but what it is, is a mirroring of behaviors, and a version of life in the complexity of it being repeated. If this was your intended message, it was loud and clear.

I didn't see anything that blatantly needed to be removed; my concern is that you remain true. Thank you for hearing and receiving what I had to say without putting me in the same context as some of the people in the book. Even with the value that you insist I added, God met **you** at the "burning bush." In writing this book, it was you who had to take your shoes off on holy grounds. I think that what you said in this day and age of candor and transparency, and keeping it 100, captured all of the criteria of truth that must be told. In conclusion, the ultimate message that you send is that what God has for you, you don't have to settle for somebody else's. You don't have to settle for attention that's sub-par. Look in the mirror and love who you see.

INTRODUCTION

On Christmas Day, 2016, I felt compelled to delete, what would have been the final chapter of one book and turn it into a book of its own. The writing experience that I had with, *Hey "Adam," "Where You At?"* was like a fresh well of water springing up that I found hard to turn off. Here it is at the end of 2020, and the same book that evolved from a tape-recorded, roundtable discussion with the late, Pastor Ruben Shannon (almost 15 years ago), has now turned into two, separate books, with a third one on the way. Since the concept of soul-mate had become such an intriguing crux of the previous investigation, the purpose of the current book is to incorporate what was a final chapter into a quick, but captivating read.

Especially rewarding for the reader who appreciates the fact that Adam was a figure of Him who was to come (Rom. 5:15), allow me to reestablish my position here. Could it be possible that Adam was engaged in covering his bride, and not preoccupied with hiding his sin? Was it truly in the name of unconditional love that God counted on the first Adam, to become willing and loving enough to leave his wonderful Paradise, just to save the woman we call Eve? Since he was the first, earthly god and Jesus was the last, human Adam, did God have any other way to demonstrate to His Son, the love between a man and his bride?

In other words, Adam, being the first, human example, was given the **man**date to expose unity and the duty of a bridegroom (Rom. 5:19a). Here are a few, other excerpts from the "Adam" book that bear repeating. Because Eve was the weaker vessel, I believe that Adam **took** the fall and **willingly** gave up his immortality in order to become her covering. Why Adam would demonstrate perfect love and give up immortality for the love of a woman was really the focus of that investigation.

Why Jesus would give up immortality and leave the Father to die on an old rugged cross is a large part of both conclusions. In order for either of them to die and save their brides from eternal damnation, they had to willfully become sin and go to hell. Evidently, when God looks at us, He sees Jesus, but when He looked at Eve, He saw Adam. Even if this biblical backdrop was written in the Bible as a parable, it makes a darn-good parallel.

Not only am I waiting on a man to spiritually love me as Christ loves the Church. When God looks at me, I need him to single out for me, the MAN who is **god-**enough to MAN-UP and marry me! If Satan breaches security for any reason, I do not expect you to leave me to myself, to fend for myself. I expect you, "Adam," to be man-enough to "eat" on purpose ("I did eat"), and then, "leave the Garden" on purpose with the woman who is now, bone of your bone and flesh of your flesh. Why? Having absorbed my true self **into** you, how can you even think of existing **without** me? I have gone way too far into the other book, but here is my calculated conclusion.

All over the world, Jesus was the Lamb, but Adam was the man because he took a stand for a woman called Eve. As far as I am concerned, somewhere on this huge planet, there is only ONE man whom my soul loveth. ***"The watchmen that go about the city found me: to whom I said, Saw ye him whom my soul loveth?"*** (Song of Sol. 3:3 KJV). That's the rationale that led me to my probing inquiry: *Why **DIDN'T** I get Married?*

Having temperaments and a history that makes me supersensitive to intrusion, I require a lot of privacy and uninterrupted time for my God-given passions. However, by the time that I am married, I want to be so whole (nothing missing, nothing broken, and nothing lacking) that I will **want** him more than I **need** him! I want your God; I want your ministry. I want your love; I want your sex. I want your protection; I want your security, but most of all, I want YOU! A godly man would rather be wanted for who he is, than for what he has to offer.

Besides, when you lead people to believe that you "need" them, you are most vulnerable to being controlled **by** them. The way that I was able to break free from a 15-year, controlling and manipulative relationship was not by being independent. It was by being "inner-dependent." That brings me to another reason why I never married. Even though I was delivered from him, I still had some scars that needed to be healed. When you are not whole, you will end up multiplying toxicity because you give each other broken pieces that neither of you were prepared to fix. My point: learn to be complete before you get connected!

It is easier to love a person until death when you have learned to love yourself to life. After learning to love myself to life, I have decided to wait on "purpose." A Boaz with purpose is better than the "Wrong-Az" with power. And, when you get rid of the "Wrong-az," God will bless you with the "Right-az." In my opinion, the reason that man came up with the term, "lawfully-wedded," is that they are just that: lawful – even if it's not spiritual. Therefore, when you learn to say, "I do" to God first, you will learn to say, "I won't" to the "Wrong-az."

With divorce not being an option, I have the expectation of getting it right the first time because I choose to wait on the right one. Anything that becomes undone is an indication that God didn't do it. Illogically, when we depend on our humanism, we end up seeking makeovers and looking for "do-overs." But if God does it the first time, it will never come undone at any time. Why DIDN'T I get Married? The man that I came out of is the man that I plan to walk back into – and the two shall become one again (read Gen. 2:23). Unless he has settled, by giving his rib to the wrong woman, he is still trying to find himself (the him in me). Married or single, this book is bound to "purpose-ize" your wait and maximize your purpose. …"Wait I say, on the Lord" (Psa. 27:14b).

CHAPTER ONE

BROKEN BUT NOT BEYOND REPAIR

"I was not only trying to find love in all the wrong places;
broken but not beyond repair,
I WAS LOOKING FOR GOD IN ALL THE WRONG PEOPLE!"
#K.DR

With so many layers to my personal story, I was really "on the fence" about inserting this chapter to a manuscript that was pretty much, written three years ago. While I dreaded opening what most would consider a "can of worms;" yet, when I reflected on my past, it has **much** to do with why I didn't get married. At 17 years old, my life was negatively impacted by an illicit relationship with a married man. Earlier, during a tumultuous time in my childhood, I became the goddaughter, while being groomed to become the mistress. Despite his profound concern as a father figure, eventually, I was lured to a hotel for a counseling session; while he claimed that it was for the sake of privacy.

The crux of the whole matter is this: the power of death and life **really** is in the tongue (Prov. 18:21). Fifteen years later, when I became bold enough to walk away from this relationship with absolutely **nothing**, he declared over my life that **nothing** good would come to me. Albeit it was 27 years ago, I remember this curse as though it was spoken yesterday. He wished above all that I would **NOT** prosper, and due to the consistent medical expenses and lack of funds that made life miserable, I either filed a Chapter 11 or Chapter 13, every few years, until I finally lost count. Losing three cars and my first home to foreclosure, I was *broken but not beyond repair.*

Until the last couple of years, I had subconsciously given him the power to create my reality. The difference between cursing and cussing, the curse continued to trigger chronic depression, and relentless sicknesses and diseases. Having taken my power back, this chapter reflects the death and burial impact of those evil words. But if you stay with me, you will see and encounter my resurrection experience.

Sad to say, demonic cults are often developed out of religious cultures. In any event, my whole assignment in any of my writings is about cleaning up a system. Consider this: God will trust you enough to give you an assignment; He will love you enough to release you from it. So until I get the release, I simply cannot ignore the plight of victims who are hurting and broken by men and women of God who use their spiritual authority to manipulate the impressionable minds of our future leaders. Current leaders, you must focus on doing right so that nobody is hurt by you doing wrong. Be defenders and not defilers, by keeping your fingerprints off God's property!

Hopefully, defending my "dissertation" and sharing this chapter leaves a lasting impression in a compelling way that shows I was just as vulnerable and human as the folks that I may be sharing with. Whether you are the victim, the accused, the abuser, or even an innocent bystander, never defend your fears by rationalizing truth with your feelings. We cannot stay in ministry trying to avoid the unavoidable. "You may not have created the problem, but it's yours to heal," says Iyanla Vanzant. We were not called to do image; we were called to bring healing. Yet, the sad reality of church leadership is that it becomes more maintenance than ministry.

Real people with real pain deserve to share their real stories with real audiences. Therefore, my only intention here is to present a brief precursor of who I was then, as it relates to where I am now. Likewise, if you have never gone through anything, how can you minister to people who have gone through everything? "Learn to critique without condemning!" (Iyanla). Even Proverbs 17:15 (NIV version) says: ***"Acquitting the guilty and condemning the innocent–the LORD detests them both."*** *Broken but not beyond repair,* let's band together around our brokenness to defend the integrity of God's name and build each other up.

In doing so, we must stop acting like scared dogs that won't bark when it's time to confront. Moving forward, we must stop normalizing sin and abuse, and realize that truth that is not known cannot set you free (John 8:32). Don't own it and slide in it, just because you got caught. Embrace it, and **stand** in your truth because of the level of grace that is in public repentance. Only then will you learn to walk in real freedom and true deliverance! Since this is the season that your secret life is no longer safe, you should refuse to speak on behalf of a God that you refuse to be delivered by. As far as the followers are concerned, how can you **be** delivered if you are under a leader who refuses to **stay** delivered?

In reaffirming my assignment and laying this foundation, you do not get the right to dictate a person's timing to expose, or even **re**-expose their story. In being one of those voices that cries for justice, stop trying to keep me in "Egypt!" As of 2020, God has shown me a preview of my "Canaan!" And for Zion's sake, I will not hold my peace. But before I peel back this first layer, allow me to focus on the chapter title, and the image of the broken heart to capture the reason why I not only appreciate God; **every** day I celebrate God for my break-through and deliverance.

Simply stated, I got tired of game. Even though the game is over, Candy Bulletin posted: "If you don't heal what hurt you, you'll bleed on people who didn't cut you." Since the Lord's strength is made perfect in weakness (2 Cor. 12:9), I must continue to share my testimony to illustrate the transforming power of transparency. In the words of my friend, Evangelist Jackie Jenkins: "I can't 'unknow' what I know."

Years ago, I was compelled to travel to Miami, Florida, to experience an effective illustration, preached by Bishop Louis Smith. In the message, *Broken But Not Beyond Repair*, the visual was set in motion by replacing a broken heart with a new heart. Then he used a doll that **looked** like she was whole to illustrate that she was really shattered on the inside, and cracked and damaged from things that you could not see from the surface. From what we could see from the audience, the exterior of the doll was beautiful. Yet, whatever she had been built to do was not working because she had been torn and broken from the **inside**-out.

After that, Bishop Smith used a toy house that "looked" like it was standing, but when he was able to take it apart, he made the point that a divided house could not stand. While we wear facades and "mask-up" to **pretend** that we are whole, everything that the bishop demonstrated had to go through the process of being placed in the Potter's hand. Because He is the Potter who has the power to put us back together again, we may be *broken, but not beyond repair.* When I informed him of this chapter, he told me about a nurse/atheist, who days before, had jumped 60 feet from the roof of his job. Just as his bones came through the skin, and arteries were damaged to the point that they had to place him in a coma, HE DID NOT DIE! God exhibited to the victim, the staff, and now my reader, that you are **never** too broken or damaged to be repaired.

Bishop Smith went on to talk about "B. E. V." i.e. a product that is "beyond economic value." In other words, the cost is more than what the product is actually worth. For example, your life is worth more than the abuse that you tolerated. Your peace is worth more than the "piece" you gave away. Whatever the case, we must be able to "LET GO AND LET GOD" replace the hoax with an anecdote. But because we are so untrained and unskilled in managing matters of the heart, we are only qualified to do "damage control," which often creates more damage.

Sodom & Gomorrah, Jezebel, Judas, and the devil himself refused to be repaired; some things must be destroyed from the **root**. While we can only see the surface and not the root, particularly when it comes to systemic, root issues, the devil makes transfers by making you the recipient of somebody else's issues. He has only been waiting for the right body and/or situation to show up. Since God knows the root cause of every generational curse, we must remember to take the thing that is beyond **our** repair, to the expert Potter who can either REPAIR, REPLACE, RESTORE or REMOVE it! Obviously, this message (which would make an incredible movie or Women's Conference message), has left an exceptional and indelible impression upon my memory. It is yet impacting the way that I have chosen to heal and reveal.

I coined a phrase that says: "When you evolve into WHO you really are, you won't mind embracing WHY you were." Even as Bishop Ronnie Webb once whispered in my ear that "exposure brings closure," the overall purpose of this chapter is to express the outcome of having processed and resurrected out of a 15-year, emotionally-abusive relationship (a heart issue that I ultimately had to place in the Potter's hand). Asking me to keep silent about what God has repaired, removed and replaced, is like saying: "I dare you to bleed on me after I shoot you."

May I share truth to power? Public figures are subject to public scrutiny. Consequently, when you do not get in front of your own narrative, somebody will take it and "weaponize" it against you. Alternatively, when you control the narrative and repent/change, people will show consideration for your truth and be more willing to forgive you. Leaders, please don't think that you can continue getting by with turning your "followers into bottoms," and not get exposed. "GAME OVER!" Grace will not defend what repentance can repair.

I can only hope that your view of this chapter is not equally-consistent with those in my past who have punctuated my writings with their habits of cynical thinking, feelings, opinions, etc. At any rate, you can spin this either way you want, but it will not take away from my experience. Allow me to digress here and address the "church folks." ***"AND SUCH WERE SOME OF YOU"*** (1 Cor. 6:11a KJV with emphasis added). ***"Don't bad-mouth each other, friends. It's God's Word, His Message, His Royal Rule, that takes a beating in that kind of talk. You're supposed to be honoring the Message, not writing graffiti all over it"*** (James 4:11 MSG Bible).

I anticipate the day when the Body of Christ also becomes the Face of Christ. For the complete back-story, please refer to my Trilogy, *From Mistress To Ministry*, which can be found at www.karenreid.org. For now, allow me to help you with understanding the phenomenon of clergy misconduct and on the degree to which the following details help to clarify my story and/or differentiate between conflicting meanings.

"M&Ms: MEMORIES & MISTAKES"

Realistically, it is difficult to have public victories and not have private shames. Jesus was really naked on the cross, and despising the shame, He had to deal with public nudeness (Heb. 12:2). So looking unto Him, the author and finisher of my faith, I am not just selling a book; I am sharing an experience. Accordingly, let's finish expediting my "baggage-claim" so that I will be free to proceed toward my anticipated destination.

Here, allow me to quickly clarify the brief claim that opened this chapter. *Broken but not beyond repair*, the serious disconnect with the authority figure in my home, and later being molested by a trusted adult, the need was created for a daddy-figure to love the little girl that had already become damaged baggage. Labeled today as "father-fractures," fortunately, the damage was not beyond repair. In the case of a vulnerable teenager who became the mistress to a trusted, church leader, this was likened to a case where men in positions of power use their influence to sculpt and groom innocent children to become participants of their lewd and vicious acts.

Particularly, when the trusted perpetrator is much older and more experienced than the victim who is already coming from places of abuse and brokenness, it adds a different dynamic to the situation. How? Having a "vet" in your corner, over your life, **and** in your ear calling you his daughter for 15 years, forces you to develop a set of skills and a series of sensitivities that suppress your better judgment.

God bless them, but let's overlook the people in the back for a moment. In using this opportunity to expand this topic for the leaders and generations coming after us, let's use this space to elevate **their** awareness. My doctoral studies and years of research reveal that pastors **unavoidably** become parent figures because of their trust and authority. Psychologically speaking, they are charged with the ethical responsibility of the parenting role. As a significant consequence, violations of these boundaries are not only rapes but also acts of incest (Rutter, 1977). Since the clergy's position incorporates both spiritual and moral authority in an environment or "forbidden zone" that is **expected** to be safe, **ANY** relationship that violates this professional boundary is considered **ABUSE** and **NOT** an affair. Please ask me why.

At its core, this is an ethical violation that is NOT considered consensual. Any sexual contact by a man in power that occurs within professional relationships is inherently exploitive of a woman's trust. (Rutter, 1977). Even though sex is often interpreted as **consensua**l on the part of the victim, the relationship is more detrimental than a relationship between two adults with an **even** power balance (Parnitzke & Freyd, 2013). Whereas it is hard to make sense of exploitation and maltreatment, just as brokenness was emphasized earlier, abuse deserves the same energy.

What starts such a literal and emotionally-bleeding cycle, as the one detailed in my Trilogy-Part One? As an 11 year-old, the family unit was neglected because the authority figure in the home had extramarital affairs and children outside of the home. Here is what happened after he returned later to establish a storefront ministry. Because he did not have the respect and the support that he felt **entitled** to, the "hated" daughter became the victim of naked beatings with razor straps and extension cords. How can any father apply discipline where he has not applied love? #father-fractures #father-wounds #father-scars

As a result of leaving home as a **virgin** with unembellished "female problems" and obvious signs of child abuse, can you see that young Karen D. Reid was honestly looking for a daddy, and not a dick. The monstrous reality is that the teenager would not remain the 17 year-old who agreed to meet at the hotel. Eventually, truth would prevail. *Broken but not beyond repair*, my former leader had some bleeding issues too. His concealed wounds were rotten enough to pollute my ability to say, "No; this is **not** what I'm looking for." Rather, that one, diabolically-designed distraction was not only intended to ultimately destroy God's plan for my life. Honestly, it began to satisfy my lower-self, as I began to create covenants and love affairs with more distractions.

Since my experiences hold a lifetime of wisdom, allow me to continue to debunk the abuse vs. affair foolishness. So that you won't be oblivious to the part of my story that sent ripples throughout my Pentecostal denomination, my early adult-hood was taken from me by the leader who was put into my life to protect me. Nevertheless, I was now bullied with Psalm 105:15 (KJV), by people with "church brain." They barked: ***"Touch not Mine anointed, and do My prophets no harm."*** Wrong interpretation! In 1 Samuel 15, the Lord's anointed, Saul (in vs. 23), was **verbally** condemned by Samuel for his **rebellion and stubbornness**.

David refused to touch Saul **physically** when he was delivered into his hand. In fact, he had the Amalakite killed for destroying Saul. Accordingly, the Bible makes it clear that to touch the anointed means to bring **physical** harm and/or death. It was NOT talking about defending the wrong against those who had been wronged. As one of the biggest misnomers in the Church, here is how church folks interpret it: "Touch not my sacred, golden calf, or I'll put God on you."

GAME OVER

It is the church-culture to remain silent and to avoid holding one another accountable for hurting our babies and ushering in the spirit of perversion. In fact, you "drop the ball" when you fail to report, confront, and protect. It's not real love to cover or hide a person's sickness; how will they ever get well? In fact, it is the spirit of error to turn a blind-eye when it comes to sin and issues that affect our generations. It is your business. While transparency is said to be the new ministry, "the way to right wrongs is to turn the light of truth upon them" (Ida B. Wells). The late Pastor Shannon was the only person who had enough courage to mediate my cause and attempt to put us on the path to working through the healing process together. And even in death, I honor him for that.

You would think that "if the healer could get more healing, he could heal more people" (Malcolm "MJ" Harris). *"To a greater or lesser degree, all healers are wounded healers. So, no, the entrance requirement to offer help does not include being perfect, whole, and pain free, but at least, while you're still wounded and bleeding, allow yourself to heal to a point where you're not hurting. Denying your own past and struggles can be quite damaging. The question is not perfection, but rather what we have done and will continue to do with our imperfections, traumas, addictions, and rough edges. Wearing them as a badge of identity or honor represents an imbalance. Simply having survived something awful or challenging does not make you an expert. Self-focused wounded people or survivors often superimpose their experiences and solutions on other victims"* (Sommers-Flanagan and Sommers-Flanagan (2007).

After having the conversation that was instigated by Pastor Shannon, and being given the opportunity to confront, my former leader never owned the gravity of the impact of his actions. Rather than saying, "I understand how you feel, or how that must have affected you," he continued (after years of denial and disregard), to justify his actions and normalize sin. Because he apologized like a narcissist, I was unable to effectively walk through my healing process because there was no true repentance. A real apology disarms the offended, and the **whole** truth puts reality to rest. Proverbs 16:18 simply refers to it as PRIDE.

Having built his brand around perfection, I gave up after that. God loved David because of how he RESPONDED to his sins/failures. He didn't REACT; he responded! Be careful for nothing; your sins could affect the future of other folks' actions, while their alarming-results become the exposure of your looming past. "Why is I-chabod (the glory has departed) written over many of our churches? One reason is that many of our churches foster a sexual environment. At the same time, God is against anyone establishing Him a house that is full unrepentance. Psalms 24:3b-4b says: ***'Who may stand in His holy place? He who has clean hands and a pure heart'...***

Although it was in David's heart to build God a house, God did not permit him to. He had fought too many wars and shed too much blood on the earth (read 1 Chron. 22:8). Rather, God chose his son, not because of nepotism or that he was next in line. Solomon, a man of wisdom, was also a man of peace and rest. You can't just cut the tree at the trunk; you need to get down to the root of your issues, and maybe even consider taking a 'slick-leave' from the pulpit" (Reid, 2010). Unrepentant sin and toxic relationships! It's time to "change the channel."

Yes, I was molested and mishandled before he came along (which was one of the reasons I gravitated toward him). But no matter who had left their "fingerprints," ultimately, he was the one who broke the seal. Yes, I have no problem with saying I was wrong, but I was the 17 year-old child; he was the 37 year-old adult. Because I chose to stay until I was 32, I am guilty of being a participant to the actions that I am humiliated by. Yet, even at 18, I had no cognitive knowledge of sex and the lasting effects of soul-ties, and as my only leader, he was obligated to influence me in the right direction.

Like Malcolm, I had to finally realize that what happened to me was not because I was fast, devious or mischievous. Those adult leaders made a **conscious** decision to violate me. It's no wonder that I never got married; I NEVER GOT HEALED! If your first introduction to sex is before you are cognitively prepared to handle it, it shapes the focus of your expectations and what you think is acceptable, even when it is not necessarily pleasant.

Furthermore, when you act out of a response to certain traumas, you learn new patterns. As a result of trauma-bonding, he perverted what love **looked** like, and I learned to pervert what love **felt** like. At the end of the day, the adult figures out how to hide his issues and advance to covering his actions, but the victim still needs a voice to expose and process those experiences. On the whole, when the church does not learn to discern the wound, it is your silence that makes you responsible. Eventually, victims will forget the words of their enemies; they will remember the silence of their friends.

I agree that leaders should feel dejected if nobody is correcting them. What it means is that they are considered not important enough to respond to wisdom. Toward this end, I was ecstatic to hear my brother-Bishop, Brandon B. Porter, make this gripping statement in a campaign dialogue: **"The Church can no longer abandon a people because they're trying to save a preacher!"** **"**P☺W!" Why not? The title does not make leaders special; it makes them more responsible. GAME OVER, Mister "Man of God!"

When wounds continue to go unhealed, undetected, or unaddressed, it will ultimately silence your influence as a leader/prophet, and during a time when your voice should be shifting regions and changing history. Just as truth and exposure have a way of bringing one's true self to light, "leading-while-bleeding" is tantamount to knowing that you are infected with a sexually-transmitted disease, but still having unprotected relations. Please stay with me as I complete my groundwork; the next three chapters are considerably shorter.

And since most will not go back to read my Trilogy, I feel compelled to share some of those practical polices that will create a safer haven for our babies. Whereas our church leaders' aspiration should be to the highest calling and mission of the Body, why are legal implications and rigid adherence to ethical and moral grandeur not relevant or evident in many of our churches? While we cling to the Bible as our guidelines for moral behavior, we also expect our leaders to operate in excellence, even as we all **practice** to become perfect!

To keep predators and perpetrators from bleeding on the church what has not been reconciled in their personal lives, here are my questions? Are you surveying the **extent** of the problem in an effort to explore ideas to **address** the problem? Are you making child abuse prevention a part of your adult/leader training and education? Are you providing outreach services to the abused victims? Since the victims want to be heard, are you engaging in dialogue that inspires trust and accountability? Are you requiring more openness from the church's hierarchy while engaging in resolution through communication between clergy and laity?

In too deep, the resistance to address these inquiries will continue to have a significant impact on future lawsuits. As these lauded positions of church leadership bring with them respect and unquestioned authority, here are my final questions: Will you continue to place people in positions without demanding accountability, and without being cognizant of the increasing seriousness of the crisis of abuse? Will you make public, a list of all-known perpetrators with the details of their violation? And, will you create church-wide policies that require background checks and denominational audits, and screening for employment and volunteer ministry? (Trilogy, Part One).

As the leader of those under your covering, you need to know the proclivities and weaknesses of other potential leaders. If they are attracted to children, they do not need to lead the youth ministry! Are you kidding me!?! Right here, my rant deserves to be on "10." If they have a proclivity to steal, why would you want them working with the church's finances? Consequently, people bring with them whatever they are attracted to, or whatever they have been attached to. Even so, (whether professional or religious), if your character put you in such a state of conflict that you feel you cannot uphold your moral obligations, and you are determined to do the opposite of what you teach, preach, or model, you should consider resigning. Point blank!

According to Lao Tzu, actions become habits, habits become character, and character becomes destiny. Hence, it is the standard of a leader to do the best, to be the best-possible example, particularly when so many are using the Bible as their standard but doing everything that contradicts it. Since the Church has been unable to circumvent some of this foolishness, God has come up with His reality check to show us that the *game is over*.

In my opinion, many of our churches had turned into stage plays, with the pastor as the director, and the musicians and praise team as the actors in front of a live audience. "Lights, camera, actions–flesh!" NO! It has to be ALL about the Master! Watch what He does in the next wave. Please don't get buried under the rubble of a rebellious house. Like God told the prophet in Ezekiel 12, who dwelled in the midst of a rebellious house: "Bring your baggage outside during the day and in their sight. Maybe they will consider how rebellious they are."

Out of obedience rather than ambition, that's precisely the purpose of this chapter. I am not here to be an accuser of the brethren. As a matter of fact, I would have preferred to remain private, but GOD called me to become public (which was my former leader's whole concern with my testimony). All the same, if we learn to keep our privacies inconspicuous, we won't have to worry about our indiscretions becoming publications.

Broken but not beyond repair, whether you made the chapter, or is an intricate part of my story, here is the redeeming factor: ***"Though he fall, he shall not be utterly cast down: for the LORD upholdeth him with His hand"*** (Psa. 37:4). Having personally been under construction and correction, I was shut down for remodeling and transformation. Man broke me, but he couldn't destroy me! I am convinced that there was no "payless-pump-wearing" competition that could walk in my "shoes!" "Ooops," I said that, right there! The details of that "Reality Show" can be found in Trilogy, Part One, as well. What I had said was: I was precut, predestined, prescheduled, prearranged, and predetermined to fit in a particular place in history that nobody else could fit but me. I was GRACED for this!

At the core of my scandal is the mere fact that I am the one that qualified for the job – yes, the job you see me doing NOW! In breaking the pattern of silent suffering, an important element to this chapter is that

I had to go through that, in order to write this! A part of my assignment is to challenge those who profess holiness, to perfect holiness. Hence, I have shifted my narrative from because of him–I was, to because HE is–I AM! If you follow the evidence, you will see that my testimony is a greater force for good. If truth be told, most of us have either been in failed marriages, abusive relationships, unnatural affairs, or broken covenants, but we cannot allow distraction to activate destruction. *Broken but not beyond repair*, the Potter wants to put all of us back together again.

When you give yourself to somebody, particularly for 15 years like I did, you give him a part of you, which makes **you** feel that you cannot live without **him**. #soul-ties But you're really grieving over the parts of you that you want back and can't get back. So it's not a sign of weakness to feel "poured-out;" it is a demonstration of power that empowers you to "power-up." You may think that you **need** him back, but what you really want is for him to give your power back. Learn to fill the void in your heart and not the one between your legs! *Broken but not beyond repair*, you must learn to love you, until you refuse to become another you. If you want to be first, learn how to be you.

Because I put my whole heart into whatever I commit myself to, I shared a type of intimacy that couldn't be returned. I'm not just talking about sex either because sex is often used by people to keep another person under their spell. Men will use their "nut butter" as a control tactic to bring you under submission. #soul-ties Likewise, man of God, just as Delilah did Samson, women will place your head in her lap and use the power of her words to keep you coming back. That's why you must consider how the most subtle act of manipulation can be used against you.

How can a man say that he loves you and hold you hostage and keep you captive at the same time, to his sinful nature. No! He is not in love with you; he loves what you can do for him and how you can make him feel. Alternatively, woman of God, how can you say you love the man whom you're placing seductive traps for in unsuspected places? Wow; Trilogy, Part One is a must read. This particular section in Chapter Eleven (Cover Your Head), goes on to explain the difference between a violating spirit and a seducing spirit. Before you get in too deep, the indicators should compel you to ask: "Should I uncover this woman's nakedness, or should I cover my head?" (Reid, 2010).

Sex involves body, mind, soul, and spirit, and the only one who deserves all of me (as a single "W. O. G."), is God. I never needed grace in the area of fornication. Rather than coming from a place of need and gratification, I indulged in sex to get what I wanted (love and support). I was not only trying to find love in all the wrong places; I WAS LOOKING FOR GOD IN ALL THE WRONG PEOPLE! Once I got my deliverance, I broke those soul-ties and engaged myself in a journey, called, SOULED-OUT!

Life is too short, and sex before marriage is too deep to revolve your world around anybody who does not revolve theirs around you. Use your grace for something else. As long as you are in love with the "Wrong-az," God cannot bless you with your Boaz. You will end up being without the Spirit-filled man that your soul needs because you are in love with the flesh-mate that your body craves for. ***"And be renewed in the spirit of your mind"*** (Eph. 4:23 KJV).

PAUSED ON PURPOSE
POSITIONED FOR THE PROMISE

Isaiah did not see the LORD until the year that Uzziah died. While he dwelled in the midst of a people of unclean lips, he had to take his eyes off of Uzziah and set his eyes on the King, the LORD of hosts. Maybe the reason that many of us have been unable to set our eyes on our king, we need to have an Isaiah experience so that the "Uzziahs" in our lives can die out. In order to qualify for our futures, we must reconcile with our past. When we are *paused on purpose and positioned for promise*, we cannot hold our reward and vice in the same hand.

I started pouring myself into producing training manuals for pastors and leaders, and as I developed this new expertise, I became inundated with traveling across the country. In my mind, I was discarding this chapter of my life and getting back to a life of normalcy. But when the pandemic hit and shut things down, the calm forced me to hear loud and clear: "You do not have the RIGHT to remain silent." My experience was still my "serpent" that I had to pick up by the "tail." A point well-taken, I learned from Bishop E. Bernard Jordan that becoming a "snake handler" gives you the ability to turn the "tail" into a stick that parts your "Red Sea." What a potent analogy and the power of cyber church! Since my "Red Sea" was God-assigned to show you how to part yours, the question is: What's the "snake" that you need to pick up by the tail?

Now positioned for promise, I am no longer depending on a man who thought he could keep a deadbolt on my mind and control the key to my future. Like Leah in the 29th chapter of Genesis, I needed a "brain-wave replacement." Leah wasn't considered tender-eyed because she was cock-eyed. Rather, she had low self-esteem and saw **herself** as ugly, in comparison to her sister, Rachael. Rather than seeing herself through the eyes of the One who created her, Leah saw herself through the man that chose her sister over her.

Being single should never be an indication that you are desperate, paranoid, or even available. Who lied to you? I am busy; I am working, and I am serving while I'm waiting. Positioned for promise and knowing who you are, you must use wisdom to get who you deserve. Most times the counterfeit shows up first, and when we fail to look at the details and read the "fine print," we end up settling for someone who is not a part of our assignment. As for me and my house, I am waiting **on** purpose, and I'm waiting on **Purpose** (THE-HE WHO WILL MAKE THE-SHE, A HAPPY-ME)! How about that for a preface to the next chapter? Now that the house is clean and my flesh is fresh, I must wait on the old-school love that comes with morals, values, honesty, and loyalty, with God as the foundation.

CHAPTER TWO

WHEN FLESH IS FRESH AND FLAMES ARE FLICKERING

"In order to keep the *flesh fresh and the flames flickering*,
I can't be the one whom you would settle with;
I must become the one whom you've been **searching** for." #K.DR

Out of all the books that I have written in the past, the one that I found most intriguing and revelatory was entitled: *Hey Adam, Where You At? Take A Stand And Be The Man.* However, this current one does not fall short of becoming the one that has amused me the most. The previous chapter drew a framework around my purpose and principles; this chapter should be a happy balance with regards to intimacy and romance.

As a starting point, I must point out that the very essence of Adam's substance was wrapped up in Eve's identity after his rib was used to form her. Since everything in the man is in the bone, she was now him, due to the fact that he was in her. It seems that in God's mind, Eve was designed to be Adam's **soul**-mate before she became his flesh-mate. In Genesis 2:7, the elements of the soul were activated. Connecting with her assignment, she was taken from his **side** to be interactive with her **soul**-mate's mind, will, emotions, imagination, and intellect. First knowing each other in the spirit, it wasn't until **after** they sinned that they knew each other in the flesh. Wow, I just had an epiphany; sin is the main entrance to a lot of inevitable exits. Close that door!

One thing that has become clearer to me is that God never woke Adam up to present Eve to him, **she** awakened him in the *spirit* through her God-given ability to be his life-support (Gen. 2:21-22). @-) In essence, as women come from the breasted/feminine side of God (El Shaddai), she connects with the life that was blown into the man. Therefore, whenever a woman initially awakens her man in the spirit, her F**L**ESH will always be F**R**ESH. When you do it God's way, there will never be anything on the "side-line" that makes the "main-course" uninviting.

After the fall of man, did you know that marriage was created to **avoid** fornication? Here, allow me to prove it to you. ***... "It is good for a man not to touch a woman. Nevertheless, to avoid fornication, let every man have his own wife, and let every woman have her own husband"*** (1 Cor. 7:1b-2 KJV). **IF** you are in a divine union, rather than a legal arrangement, your sexual desire will be <u>strictly</u> toward your mate. To say the least, he shall have NO NEED OF SPLIL (read Prov. 31:10-11). "Zion, what's the matter now?"

Relationships should never revolve around flesh. Ask me why. Flesh was NEVER a precursor to Adam and Eve becoming soul-mates. Whereas sin/flesh had not yet entered the world, they became spiritually-connected before they were ever physically-attracted. As Adam and Eve were the true "match made in Heaven," some people negate the possibility of finding their soul-mate because they choose to settle for a flesh-mate (people that look good and/or make you feel good). Obviously, so many relationships mirror the unfortunate statistic that playmates may eventually lead to roommates, but they may never make good soul-mates. #temporaryfix

A hint to the wise is sufficient: physical attraction is not a definite indication of a soul-mate connection. But if your focus and intentions are uniquely spiritual, God will connect you to the person who is exclusively-suited for you in the natural. This will be the person who will give you all you want because he or she will be "all-that" you have ever needed. A virtuous and righteous couple who is wholesome in character will make a much healthier marriage than a gorgeous wedding with an attractive couple who is unequally-yoked and not ready for marriage.

When I heard one pastor challenge the concept of soul-mate marriage across the pulpit, I thought, "Don't make me waiver in my faith because you refus**ed** to wait. Just because you did not marry your soul-mate and remain frustrated much of the time, it does not mean that I can't marry mine." I'm not looking for just a man whom I can live with; I'm **waiting** on that one man that I can't live without! I want us to remain so deeply in love that every anniversary will be as fresh as the original honeymoon. In order to keep the *flesh fresh and the flames flickering*, I can't be the one whom you would settle with; I must become the one you've been **searching** for.

Medical research suggests that there are approximately 208 bones in an adult's body. Clearly, it would seem that since the woman was taken from the rib, the man is now missing a bone, while the woman is walking around with an extra rib. However, I discovered that the ribs have amazing regenerative powers. This would mean that Adam's loss was only temporary, allowing him to go back to God's original design of having 24 ribs. This proves that a spiritual connection is always an addition to your life, rather than a subtraction. Allegorically, when the man has not found his true soul-mate, he is unfinished until the woman who was fit for his rib-bone is connected to the right side. Unfinished but yet whole, there was never lack in Adam. Eve was just sent to complement his wholeness.

Since "y'all" say, "opposites attract," how will you know that you have married your soul-mate and not just another flesh-mate? Well, if everything that was in his bone is now in you, you will have many of the same desires, some of the same appetites, similar visions, compatible temperaments, well-matched character traits, and even your genetic make-up should reflect one another. Thus, to a greater degree, you will think alike, believe alike, talk alike, and act alike. I really cannot see myself with anyone who is a total opposite of me. That's ludicrous and why I could not settle for any of the *False Alarms* that you will read about in Chapter Seven. From the men whom I refer to as my "false alarms," it was difficult to be companionable because we were never compatible.

Because Eve was fastidiously made for Adam, everything that he needed to survive, God put it in her. He knew that what was in her was good for him, just as what was in him was good for her. If He had made them totally opposite of each other, Adam may have welcomed the opportunity to kick Eve out of his "house." Or, he may have left the Garden without her because his "search engine" may have kicked in. "Hey Eve, 'where you at'?" Girlfriend, *fresh flesh* is the "dessert" that you bring to the table, but it is through your spiritual virtue that you pump life into your man's ego and into his life goals.

Notwithstanding, nothing else moved Adam like Eve did – not even the serpent. Both connected and attracted to her spirit of intimacy (in-to-me), they never thought about sex until after they sinned. *-* Celibacy is easy when sex becomes mind over matter. I established in my previous writings that once she came on the scene, they were unable to live without the other. As he was by her side, even in the midst of the most life-altering decision ever in history, he loved everything about her because he loved himself. And since he loved the-HIM who gave him, him-self (Eve), everything about him was perfect for her.

Many people have been married multiple times, or are completely miserable in the marriage because they are trying to make it work for the children's sake. Or, they are trying to make it last for the church's sake. 3 John 1:2 KJV (with emphasis added) says, ***"Beloved, I wish above all things that thou mayest prosper and be in health, even as thy soul*** [mind, will, emotions and intellect] ***prospereth."*** Man, your soul can't prosper when your rib is connected to the wrong woman! If the woman that you have found is not good for you, you do not have the approval or favor of the LORD (Prov. 18:22). Woman, your soul won't prosper either, when your life is under the wrong "**HEAD**ing."

God never expected us to go through multiple relationships in order to find the right mate. I believe that Bishop Earl Carter popularized this phrase or one that's similar: "If God intended for us to have multiple partners, when He opened Adam's side, He would have pulled out a whole slab, not just one rib." If you have physical lust for someone else, and you find yourself tripping, tipping, and dipping, the woman you're with may belong to another man's rib.

Moving forward, the priority should not be based on flesh or "fresh meat!" Woman of God, take the time to wait and allow the man to search for you! Man of God, take the time to pray, and seek God for favor! The key to your success is the FAVOR on your wife! "If your soul is bitter and toxic because you chose the wrong wife, how can you prosper? How can you be free to think your best thoughts? You won't even have the needed energy to fight off disease. Rather, all of your energy is being expended into the chaos that you are living in. It's no wonder why some men work all of the time. You don't have the focus to win because all of your energy is going into fighting something that is competing with your success.

You could be arguing with someone who may never bend, so you should not base your decision to marry around the hopes of changing him, or her for that matter. Consistent with dumpaday.com, the only way you can change a man is if he wears a diaper. For myself, I refuse to attempt to change a person, especially one that's set in their ways. Why would I operate my heart from another person's head, or control my emotional thermostat from another person's mind? When we pray God's will to be done in earth, just as it is in heaven (Mt. 6:10b), what's going on in heaven should reflect what is going on in our lives. Stop praying about the fruit, and curse it at the roots. The fruit is **what** we do; the root is **why** we do it.

The Children of Israel pitched tents, but they never built houses. Never build a house where you were never meant to stay. Never turn on the utilities where you know you're bound to leave. Have you built a house in your desert? Have you built a house in your pain? Have you developed a pathology or built a coping mechanism for the way you think about yourself, asked Bishop Jakes (2016)? If you answered yes to any of these questions, now you know why the flesh is no longer fresh, or the flames are no longer flickering. In concurrence with Rehab Time, "Don't let the person who don't love you keep you from the person who will." #MovePastYourPAST It's never too late to ask God for a turnaround, or pray for the grace to facilitate a reset.

CHAPTER THREE

IF YOUR "BOO" IS NOT YOUR BOAZ, YOU MAY HAVE MARRIED THE "WRONG-AZ"

"I have accepted the fact that sometimes, God saves the best for last – the 'Best-az' for the 'Last-az'! In my circle of friends and family, I am definitely last, but I still have class, with my **'Classy-Crazy-az!'** Before I will marry an 'Unemployed-Az,' I'll work my 'Own-az'." L☺L #K.DR

Warning! THIS chapter is surely not for the super-spirituals or pseudo-religious. If you decide to move forward at your own risk, keep an open mind, and don't judge me. For those who choose to judge me, pray that I become as perfect as you. So, in the book of Ruth, Boaz was a mighty man of wealth; he was a man that was handsome, spiritual, and sensitive. "My man!" The difference in "Boaz" and the "Wrong-az" is in how they treat you. Boaz appreciates you; The "Wrong-az" abuses you! Boaz is into God; the "Wrong-az" is into himself! Boaz loves the Word; the "Wrong-az" loves the world! Boaz is a giver; the "Wrong-az" is a taker! As long as you are holding on to the "Wrong-az," you will never attract the "Right-az!"

A landowner, who invited the humble widow, Ruth, to eat regularly with him and his workers, Boaz left grain for her to claim, while he kept a "protective" eye on her. Because of his redeeming factors, through marriage she was restored from poverty, death, and the curse. However, if you want Boaz's payday, like Ruth, you must be willing to work in Boaz's field. Boaz is not going to be attracted to a "lazy-az." Because of how I carry myself, I walk and dress like I know who I am. Rarely am I hounded by a "Bozo," the clown, or "Boo-boo," the fool.

There has to be something that is so outstanding about your energy, ethics, efforts, and endeavors, that will make the right Boaz pass over thousands of other women, just to be married to you. Consistent with Mark Moore, "it was God's favor that allowed Ruth to be in Boaz's field, but it was Naomi's strategy that got her married." Think about your approach and your advances, the next time you feel tempted to wonder why it's taking so long for your God-appointed, Boaz to show up. In the meantime, if you get your soul **right**, you may meet your soul-**mate**.

Since Jentezen Franklin was bold enough to talk about the "Boaz family tree," at Pastor John Hagee's, Cornerstone Church (one of the most conservative churches in America), I feel safe to go ahead and publish it here. "While waiting on your Boaz, don't settle for any of his relatives: Broke-az, Po-az, Lying-az, Cheating-az, Dumb-az, Drunk-az, Cheap-az, Locked-up-az, Good-for-nothing-az, Lazy-az, and especially his third, distant cousin, Beating-yo-az. Wait on your Boaz and make sure he respects Yo-az!"

"Coming from the other side of the tracks," that was good, Jentzen Franklin. But since I have the "floor" now, I may as well help you out by putting my BLACK-girl-spin on it. You left out, distant cousins, "Down-low-az," "Drugged-out-az," "Controlling-Yo-az," and "Manipulating-Yo-az." In my book, these are the other "crazy-azzes" that you may want to stay "Yo-az" away from! %-) Furthermore, any "Jack-az" who does not want to work and provide for his family is a total "SORRY-AZ!" Lastly, if he is beating "Yo-az," he is "sho-nuff" a "Punk-az" that needs somebody to whip "**His**-az!" Like I warned you on the cover: *Either Boaz, or "NO-Az" at all.*

Paradoxically, I have accepted the fact that sometimes, God saves the best for last – the "Best-az" for the "Last-az"! L☺L In my circle of friends and family, I am definitely last, but I still have class, with my "Classy-Crazy-az!" I am having way-too much fun with this. %- I may be a hopeless romantic, but if I can help you get to where I'm trying to go, when my time comes, I will remember how you got you there. Meanwhile, I will continue to wait on a mutual, divine attraction and he who will fill my unclaimed presence with a sense of meaning and *purpose.*

I am reminded of a situation where I cautioned someone that her "sorry-az," "no-good-az," "ugly-az" boyfriend had sent me an inappropriate text. I was really trying to protect "her-az" because I knew that she deserved better. Consequently, I wasn't sure if she believed that I was totally innocent or not. At any rate, I was so detached from this "zero-az" of a Boaz that I would have rather wiped "my-own-az" with a razor blade than be his girlfriend with a simple headache.

At least, the situation with the "ugly-az" forced me to read my own resume, which at minimum, made me realize that my self-worth was much larger than my self-esteem. So after taking a good look in the mirror, I could not believe, that by any stretch of the imagination, how, why, or if my character was even questionable with someone like "his-az." "Yikes!" No matter what my taste is in men as opposed to the next person, here is my point: compromising with the "devil's-az" is like signing a contract with death.

"For real-in real life," I was once introduced to a celebrity producer who offered me $100,000 (not to help promote my projects), but to commit to being his sex partner whenever he came into town. On a another occasion, I was offered $5,000 from a local preacher who asked me for a one-time, sexual escapade. These were propositions that spoke to areas of brokenness in my life. Consequently, this was at a time when that amount of money would have prevented me from losing my home, filing another bankruptcy, **and** it would have been enough to make me debt-free. Guess what: I REFUSED BOTH OF THEM. "Just say N☹!".

As a woman of God, I recognized that He had a proper passage that prohibited unethical propositions that would lead to ungodly partnerships. Here is the "kicker." Because I refused to compromise, I was blessed with over $150,000, not long afterwards. That proves that the blessing was inevitable, but it was not God's plan and definitely not His practice. Not only do I refuse to lower my standards for "jokers;" clearly, no amount of $-$ can make me compromise my peace, my integrity, or my divine relationship for money, fame or fortune.

Oh, by the way, *if your "Boo" is not your Boaz, you likely married the "Wrong-az."* Still single and technically homeless at that point (2017), I had four marriage proposals from **professional** men who could have all given me the security that I so desperately needed. The questions I asked: Will I be in the will of God? Will they become a "Boo" who can provide prosperity, or should I continue to wait on the Boaz that will maximize my *purpose*? One of them even proposed to transfer his job to accommodate any place I chose to live. He offered to build me a home, twice the size of the one that he had recently built for himself.

Oh, I definitely gave some thought to it; I am not foolishly-single like some may presume. Before there is a level of attachment though, there has to be a level of attraction. Remember also that compatibility must precede companionability. And, where there is no affection, there won't be much commitment. How can you **submit** to one another if you are not **committed** to each other? Along these lines, I am still single because I have not experienced all of these elements with one, single person. Not only do I want the best for me, but if I am demanding the best **from** him, I must commit to being the best **for** him. Woman of God, please don't miss that!

Question: Since so many married couples are unhappily-attached, why is there such a concern for the singles who are happily-unattached? I don't get it. I am not miserably-single, so why should I compromise my standards to become miserably-married? "Hooking-up" with someone for only what they can do for me would be telling God that I don't trust Him enough to wait on my soul-mate. Oh, I had to come back on the day of this 2nd submission (at 4:00 in the morning) and find some space for this one, last edit.

You will find many relationship realities in this book that need to be taught, particularly to our young, single-**pregnant** ladies. Give them other solutions **beyond** marrying their baby-daddy, just because the Church has taught us that it's the thing to do. In many cases, marriage is only a means to an end. When sex become stale and new babies grow older, some good daddies will make bad husbands. Don't put yourself in double jeopardy (marriage and misery), just because you made a mistake. Marriage is not for immature people! Immature people have random sex and make innocent babies. Mature people get married, make love, and raise godly children (in that order).

Teach our young people that the difference between obsession, possession, fascination, and infatuation are the REAL facts of life. Since this is the only chapter with some extra space at the end, this is a good place to add one more edit before they take away my "mic.". To all of you "slick-Ricks" and "Casanovas" out there: sometimes you can't help who you fall in love with; just **stop** trying to love more than one person at the same time. wink-wink:,-) And remember that a woman's intuition is often accurate.

Okay, keep reading. Once your life is touched by someone who is going in the direction of your destiny, that is the person who will make the difference in your distance. The distance must be worth the difference! Your destiny-partner is the person who will make your comfort-zone uncomfortable, and the person who will make you discontent with being content. Learn to follow the progressive voice of God, and remain cordial without getting connected. *If your "Boo" is not your Boaz, you may have married the "Wrong-az."*

Whereas some people are still holding onto my past, my "thorn had a point to it." Interestingly, I discovered that thorns did not grow upon the earth until **after** the fall of man. Yet, God has taken a curse and used it as the crowning agent of salvation. What a powerful revelation from my brother-Bishop Brandon Porter. The point of the *thorn* is that I didn't just **com**e through my 15-year relationship; I **evolved** through that. I even feel safe to say that it was more prophetic than it was personal. How can I say that when it involved other individuals? "Destiny is not about a person; it is about a people," adds Bishop Porter.

Thus, in this season of my life, you do not EVER have to worry about me missing my Boaz over a "jack'd-up-az" – "knock-off," or "throwback," that belong to "somebody-else's-az." The only triangle that I'm getting involved in is the Father, the Son and the Holy Ghost! Furthermore, an "upgrade" from what I am even accustomed to is nothing less than "First-Class," "Five-Star," "Gold-Crown," "Diamond," or "Platinum." Even though I am a "limited-edition," I am not waiting because I'm on "stand-by." I am waiting because I can **afford** to wait. God has afforded me priority access to some favors that have its advantages, **outside** of being married.

In general, many of us are on the same "plane" but not in the same class. Whether you are flying solo or not, the way to know that you are in "first-class" is if you're eating "steak on a plate." If you are on the "economy side of the curtain" and keep attracting "Bozo" instead of Boaz, you need to upgrade your standards in the direction that you aspire to go. Leveling-up is refusing to settle for "ground-transportation." A part of faith is letting go of what you had in mind and being open to the destiny-connection that God has in store.

When you evolve, the question that you must keep in mind is: "Will the person I choose be able to evolve with me and become a good fit for my future? "Bozo," who "ain't" even "Boo-worthy," can only afford "peanuts and pretzels." Seriously, never give a man your "dessert" who can't afford to buy you "lunch." When what you crave is not CHANGED, you must change what you want so that you can attract who you need!

In conclusion, you should never allow your personal insecurities to make you misjudge another "sistah" because you are intimidated by the same respect that **you** deserve. The issue is not the other woman; "iss-ue." Well, in some cases, the issue may be "the other woman." Just make sure that you are not one of those "silly women" that I write about in the next chapter. At any rate, I hope that I have not been offensive, but the crux of my "shade" is to convince you that you are worth so much more than what you may be settling for. So "level up," Queen. The change may cost some ceaseless adjustments, but at the end of the day, the results will be a reflection of some limitless advantages.

CHAPTER FOUR

"50 SHADES" OF SILLY WOMEN

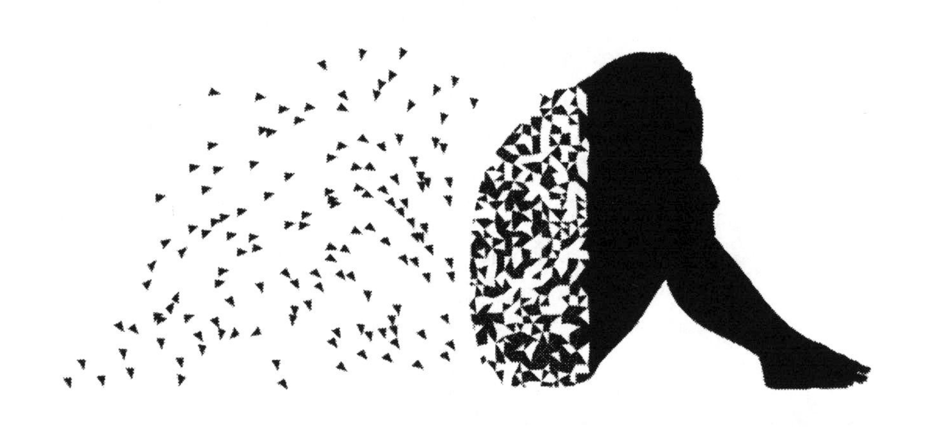

"For of this sort are they which creep into houses,
and lead captive SILLY WOMEN
laden with sins, led away with divers lusts"
(2 Tim. 3:6 with emphasis added).

DIFFICULT TIMES AHEAD
2 Timothy 3:1-9 (MSG Bible)

"Don't be naive. There are difficult times ahead. As the end approaches, people are going to be self-absorbed, money-hungry, self-promoting, stuck-up, profane, contemptuous of parents, crude, coarse, dog-eat-dog, unbending, slanderers, impulsively wild, savage, cynical, treacherous, ruthless, bloated windbags, addicted to lust, and allergic to God. They'll make a show of religion, but behind the scenes they're animals. Stay clear of these people.

These are the kind of people who smooth-talk themselves into the homes of unstable and needy women and take advantage of them; women who, depressed by their sinfulness, take up with every new religious fad that calls itself 'truth.' They get exploited every time and never really learn. These men are like those old Egyptian frauds Jannes and Jambres, who challenged Moses. They were rejects from the faith, twisted in their thinking, defying truth itself. But nothing will come of these latest imposters. Everyone will see through them, just as people saw through that Egyptian hoaz."

THE "50 SHADES"

1. **Silly:** Since this "shade" is so specific to my past situation, and I have both reference and experience on it, let me began here: One way to know that your "Boo" is not your Boaz, AND that you are a "silly woman," is that you allow a married man to take advantage of your "goods" for cheap or free, while the wife whom he criticizes to you, still get the benefits. Tell him this: "Whomever you spend your money on, buy cars, houses, and flowers for, that's who you need to get your sex from. Don't play me for a 'cheap-az' thrill. My value is far above rubies."
2. **Needy**: you are co-dependent, which makes you an easy target for witchcraft and manipulators who want to take advantage of you.
3. **Distracted:** you just want a man, whether he has a relationship with God or not; it does not matter, as long as he has one with you.

4. **Desperate:** you will have sex on the first date because you feel that sex will provoke him to ask you out on second date.
5. **Smothering:** you call him more than he calls you because you think that you can actually keep track of his whereabouts.
6. **Stupid:** you go to work while he lays up at your house because you are willing to cover a man who refuses to work, while he is trying to avoid paying child support for babies by someone else. But at least you got a man, right?
7. **Dim-witted:** you give him your income tax check; that keeps him **close** for a **few** days.
8. **Brainless:** instead of providing you three meals a day, you are silly enough to allow him to beat you for breakfast, lunch and dinner.
9. **Intimidated:** just to avoid being alone, you will allow him to control and manipulate your "thermostat" – temperaments, moods, and actions.
10. **Dumb:** you continue having babies, trying to manipulate him into marrying you.
11. **Foolish:** you know he is sleeping around, but you refuse to let him go.
12. **Risk-taker:** you would rather take a chance on STDs, than to sleep in an empty bed.
13. **"Slow-as-a-Crockpot:"** he's over 40 and has never owned his own home, but you never gave it a second thought to ask why has he digressed rather than progressed.
14. **Irresponsible:** not only does he refuse to work, but when he does work, he can't keep a job, but you cover him.
15. **Idiotic:** you are aware that he's bi-sexual, but at least he's having sex with you.
16. **Unwise:** he does not treat his mother and/or sister like ladies, so you don't even expect him to treat you like one.
17. **Oblivious:** he refuses to pay child support, but you think he will make a better father to your children than the children he ignores.
18. **"Dizzy-Daisy:"** he would rather gamble his money away than provide for the home, but you persist in taking up the slack.
19. **Hopeless-Romantic:** you want to establish a family, but he refuses to establish a relationship; you continue to pursue him.

20. **Clueless:** you want to marry him, but he doesn't want to marry you; yet, you refuse to move on, making it easier and easier for the "clean-up woman" to take your place.
21. **Miserable:** he has violent tendencies, and/or he abuses you emotionally, physically, and verbally, but you stay anyway.
22. **Careless:** you know he is a drug dealer, and rather than choosing to be let him go, you tolerate him selling drugs out of your house.
23. **Pathetic:** he has a substance abuse problem, but it doesn't matter; as long as he's there and taking out his drunkenness on you.
24. **Appalling:** he has terrible hygiene issues, but a stinky/nasty man is better than no man.
25. **Indulging:** he has no respect for your house rules; but you want him to show-up anyway.
26. **Fearful:** you shower him with gifts, while he showers you with abuse.
27. **Long-suffering:** he is a habitual criminal, but you tolerate a jailbird than no man at all.
28. **Timid:** he never shows you affection or attention, but rather than be without a man, his presence is enough to make you content with being the "unsung hero."
29. **Tolerant:** he refuses to respect you in private and ignores you in public.
30. **Dutiful:** you persist in doing wifely duties at girlfriend's prices.
31. **Overly-Submissive:** he does not own a car, but he refuses to pump your gas; you acquiesce to pumping your own gas.
32. **Aggressive:** you have to "key" his shoe because he doesn't own a car.
33. **Compliant:** you are content with his hair and nails looking better than yours.
34. **Accommodating:** you allow him to give you romance without any finance.
35. **"Blind-as-a-Bat:"** being cremated is his only hope for a "smoking" body, but you think ugly is the new norm.
36. **Ignorant:** you turn a "blind eye" to the "red flags" and believe that you can change him into being who you want.
37. **In-Denial:** you make excuses for being treated horribly; you would rather ignore the fact that you are the only one who can change it.

38. **Overly-Lenient:** you will allow a man to walk all over you, but will accept, "I'm sorry," as a simple answer to making up for all the times that he refused to sincerely apologize.
39. **Docile:** you are willing to become a full-blown dummy to someone who has taken control over every decision and aspect of your life.
40. **Optimistic:** I may get my "church card" revoked with this one, but you tolerate him coming to your house to shower, shave, shit and have sex.
41. **Hopeful:** you keep posting him, but he won't post you. Shawn Henderson says: "Y'all not Post-To-Be-Together."
42. **Coward:** he calls you his angel, but you are satisfied to live in hell.
43. **Lonely:** his presence literally frustrates you, but to avoid sleeping alone at night, you refuse to adjust to his absence.
44. **No-self-worth:** you know that he's damaging you for the next relationship, but to keep him as long as possible, you are content with building him up for the next woman.
45. **Hasty:** you know that you are unequally-yoked, but you would rather compromise your standards and take a chance on being together anyway.
46. **Spineless:** you allow him to discipline your children without applying love.
47. **Low-Self-Esteem:** he continues to make you feel unattractive, and you believe him.
48. **Overly-Confident:** Finally, the subject of divorce is such an important topic that the next chapter will be given to it totally. A few thoughts will be sufficient at this time. Here we go: he refuses to finalize his divorce, but you allow him to keep "stringing" you along, thinking that he's really going to marry you. Really?
49. **Obsessed:** when he tells you the **LIE** that he loves you, you reply: "I love you more."
50. **GUILTY-OF-ABUSE-BY-ASSOCIATION!!!!** You are aware that he violates and sexually-abuse your children, but you ignore it, and cover-up for him.

Side-note: Israel came out of Egypt, but they grumbled and complained about being FREE, and literally wanted to go back ☹. Many people love bondage because it is **easier** than being free. Why? When you are in prison, you are told when to eat, sleep, and wake-up. Alternatively, when you are free, you have to make **decisions**, AND be accountable for your choices. The purpose of displacement is proper placement, but you must make the decision to get out and not go back!

KEEP THE MESSAGE ALIVE:
2 Timothy 3:12-17 (MSG Bible)

"Anyone who wants to live all out for Christ is in for a lot of trouble; there's no getting around it. Unscrupulous con men will continue to exploit the faith. They're as deceived as the people they lead astray. As long as they are out there, things can only get worse. But don't let it faze you. Stick with what you learned and believed, sure of the integrity of your teachers–why, you took in the sacred Scriptures with your mother's milk! There's nothing like the written Word of God for showing you the way to salvation through faith in Christ Jesus. Every part of Scripture is God-breathed and useful one way or another–showing us truth, exposing our rebellion, correcting our mistakes, training us to live God's way. Through the Word we are put together and shaped up for the tasks God has for us."

CHAPTER FIVE

"DIVORCE COURT"

The #K.DR commentary on Mark 10:9: "Maybe that's why God only took the right rib and left the other, so that if you gave the **right** one to the **wrong** woman, you would still have the **left** one to give to the **right** wife."

"Divorce court" is finally in session. "God, moving forward, please help me to maintain continuity with minimum interruption in procedures." To begin with, if you cannot stand one another and you are just tolerating instead of celebrating, clearly, your marriage is **not** a "match-made-in-heaven." Basically, any marriage that is not a mirror of your right relationship with God, and your commitment to God is not outwardly reflected in your commitment to each other, then, you did not make a great choice.

In your relationship, can you "name that tune?" Was it: *Take me to the King*, or, *Take me to see "Judge Ma-**bal**-lene."* To circumvent ending up in *divorce court*, never develop a family before establishing a relationship. Without a doubt, the Father does not design anything for our ultimate destruction, divorce, demise, or even, decrease. In other words, He would never ordain something that is out of order, or that would create chaos. He wouldn't even "hook you up" with anybody that's going to break you down, or destroy everything that you have ever worked for. Sometimes, to avoid becoming a "reality show," you just need to say, "N☹."

That's why Mark 10:9 KJV (with special emphasis) says: ***"What therefore GOD hath joined together, let not man put asunder."*** If man puts you together, then, man has the jurisdiction and the justification to put you asunder. And guess what: a divorce could be justified. "Ooops!" While I explicate my disclaimer, may we go ahead and acknowledge the "elephant in the room" because I am about to step on some **sanctified-Holy-Ghost-filled** toes! Disclaimer: No matter what advice anyone gives you about **your** relationship, **always** follow the progressive voice of the GOD. ***"In all thy ways acknowledge Him, and He shall direct thy paths"*** (Prov. 3:6 KJV).

Now that we have a mutual understanding, here is the "K.DR" commentary of the above Scripture, Mark 10:9. "Maybe that's why God only took the right rib and left the other, so that if you gave the **right** one to the **wrong** woman, you would still have the **left** one to give to the **right** wife." "Ha!" This is going to be a fun chapter too. On a serious note, God does not even recognize what He did not authorize. Or, maybe I should say, He is not **obligated** to sustain what He did not ordain. "Abraham," if you are expecting the right return, you had better make another "deposit," or you may end up receiving something that was NOT **promised**.

I am aware of Byonce's song: *If you like it put a ring on it.* However, a ring may not amount to a "nickel's worth of dog's meat" IF, God did not join the two together. He may honor it just because He gave man dominion in the earth, but a legal action does not obligate Him to prosper it. **I would much rather be in a spiritually-authorized covenant than a legally-recognized contract.** #powerful! Since I have my "mic" back, let me say this loud and clear: THE RIGHT TO SAY, "I"M HAPPY!" TRANSCENDS THE ABILITY TO SAY, "I DO!"

Oh my God, I feel the Anointing on this chapter already! Get ready; here comes another powerful nugget! THE PERSON THAT HAS THE CAPACITY TO MAKE YOU HAPPY SHOULD ALSO BE THE PERSON WITH THE ABILITY TO INSPIRE YOU TO STAY **HOLY**. Otherwise, you may need to padlock the "door" from the man who ended up putting a ring on "it." "Judge Ma-**bal**-lene," you said that! "You gone-work 'wit' me?" Here is the crux of the matter: if she is not your help-meet before you put the ring on "it," she will not meet God's standard of an ideal wife – not **after** the ceremony has ended, nor, while she is walking around with your ring on her finger. ***"My soul waiteth for the Lord"...*** (Psa. 130:6 KJV). Instead of putting a ring on "it," you better **wait** on "it!" ***... "Wait I say, on the LORD"*** (Psa. 27:14b KJV).

God gives you your wife long before the courts give you a marriage certificate. You just can't choose the one you "FEEL;" you have to FIND the one who has your FAVOUR (Prov. 18:22). When God brought Eve to Adam, there was never a ritual or a ceremony. When he woke up, he must have said: "Ooops, there it is." That's why it is important to enter into the mind of Christ. When you are renewed in the spirit of your mind (Eph. 4:23), you will think from His perspective. Then, in desiring the things of GOD and having the mind of Christ (1 Cor. 2:16), we will know what to look for, who to avoid, what to wait on, and WHO we should live with.

Here is my theory: since God knows where I am at any given time, and He knows where the man is that He has put to sleep to specifically wake up to me, HE has the capability and enough wisdom to make our paths cross. Why should I have to look for a man online, and pay a fee for what Jesus died to give me for free? According to Proverbs 3:5-6, all I need to do is TRUST in the LORD with all my heart; and lean not unto my OWN, inadequate understanding. And, in **all** my ways acknowledge Him, and

He SHALL (in His own timing) direct my paths. In the **mean**time, I am determined to remain content in the state I'm in!

You will never find me anxious and impatient when it comes to being single. I am too busy becoming "**inner**-dependent" and finding out what God has invested on the **inside** of me. If there is **not** such a man for such a time as this, "I would much rather be alone, than to be married wrong." In the words of Pastor Ed Rhino, "Your purse stands a better chance alone with a crack- head than you do with the wrong man!" I have come this far by faith **without** a man; therefore, I refuse to be one of those silly women who will take any man, just to say, "I got a man." Young lady, you should not be lurking around on the internet **looking** for a man! The woman waiteth, and the man findeth! ***"Whoso findeth a wife findeth a good thing" ...*** (Prov. 18:22 KJV).

Just as my dad has been preaching to me lately about being careful not to attach myself to "wild spirits," you may end up with something that your pastor can't pray away. Until you become **comfortable** with being alone, you may never know if you are choosing someone out of love, or entirely out of loneliness. Bishop Jakes (2016) pointed out in *Crazy Choices* that sometimes you have to be comfortable with the empty seat or the empty bed. Alone in an empty bed is far better than being in it with the wrong person. Personally, I would rather be in the class of loneliness than to fill the empty seat with the wrong man. I think it safe to say that most times, our way is not always God's will.

Love is said to be blind, but marriage is an eye-opener. To illustrate the fundamental principles of this entire chapter, allow me to offer a classic scenario that is very personal and sensitive to me; it may be true-to-life for others, as well. My dad, who was married for over 50 years to my poor, miserable (now deceased) mother who regretted the day she ever met him, recently made an eye-opening confession to me. For 18 years, he had been the caretaker for a young lady who was physically-disabled **and** mentally-disturbed. Even though her care was contracted through the State, he literally cared for her like he was caring for a baby.

He washed her feet regularly, cooked her meals daily, made her medical appointments weekly, did her shopping often, and got him a "piece" at some points during the process. All of that just gave me a headache. (({..})) To say the least, he did "the most." He did everything for her that my sister and I wished he had done for our mother, especially, when she became terminally-ill. Ultimately, what my father demonstrated to us is that he could have done better by our mother. As a consequence of this reality, some of my siblings carry a large reserve of resentment toward him, as it relates to these family matters.

Whereas the young lady that he was caring for, passed away in the last few years, I never witnessed my him grieve over anyone to the extent that he grieved over her. I am talking literal tears. Here is the clincher: "You cannot be good enough for everybody, but you will always be the best for the one who deserves you" (Baisden Live's Photo). "Did you hear what I had just said?" Even as I witnessed my mom literally turn the other cheek once (so that she could be slapped again), what I realize now is that **he** was **not** GOOD enough for the one who deserved his best. He was only the best for the woman who required less than the best – the one that he ended up with his, *for better or for worse.*

At 78 years old at the time, he admitted that if God had healed his friend (who was almost 30 years his senior), he would have married her. Even so, I could not hold this decision against him because obviously, he loved her with an **unconditional** love. Unfortunately, he married my mom before he **found** his soul-mate, and his soul-mate passed away before he could marry her. "In everything give thanks;" otherwise, I wouldn't be here to discuss the decision that brought the division. After he missed out on marrying the **disabled soul-mate**, he ultimately ended up with a **disturbed wife** whom he claimed tried to poison him. #RiskedBeingPoisoned2GetAnotherPiece

Sixty years ago, our parents knew nothing about soul-mates, or praying and waiting on God for a spouse that was the most compatible. Based on emotions and hormones, most marriages turned into commitment due to Christianity. A few turned into love due to longevity. Others turned into convenience because of the children. They did not understand that you build partnerships with people you respect, but you marry the person you love, until death do you part.

Here is something else that our parents were unaware of. Because of their union, the plan of God should have been **accelerated** in the earth. Whenever soul-mates connect, even people **outside** of the relationship get blessed. You give birth to miracles that would have otherwise been impossible. If God had blessed me with my soul-mate while I still **desired** to give birth, I had planned to believe for a miracle baby, even though it was medically-impossible. On the contrary, and as a custom, our parents wanted to have sex, so they married the first person whom they felt attracted to and could get some attention from. They never investigated the family tree to see where and what the roots led to (why people are born to do "what the hell" they do). We need to know the lineage of the family's matriarch and who you were raised by, so we can figure out who's at fault. Crazy begets crazy, but it does not mean that I have to marry "Crazy!"

It did not even matter to our mothers what skills the man had, or if he would be a consistent provider in the future. The only thing that mattered is: I feel like I'm in love, so to stay in the church – "thus saith the Lord," I think you are the one. They likely went ahead and had sex outside of marriage (some of them getting more tail than the toilet seat). So**,** they got married, had more sex, made babies, made bills, paid bills, had more babies, and raised children. They remained either, happy or unhappily ever after, until they died or ended up in *divorce court.*

On reflection, here is what was so disheartening to me about my family's scenario. As far as I am aware of, our mom tolerated his infidelity and neglect as a result of four, other women and three, additional children, during what was considered the prime of her life. As Black women, we don't just stand by our men; we carry them **and** cover for them. How can a woman cover a man who does not think enough of her to cover his cheating penis? Why do men cheat, anyway? In my opinion, some enjoy the variety-effect (the "all-you-can-eat-salad bar/buffet-cheaters"), while others crave for the freaking-attention that they don't get at home.

Wife, that's why I promote being a "lady on the streets but a freak in the sheets" (lyrics by Monye147). Either way, some men will be "dogs," no matter what you do. Why? Dogs have no conscious; they will eat until they make themselves sick. And sometimes, they will bite the hand that feeds them. "Adam," why would you hurt yourself, when what's in you is in her? She carries your name because she is a re-presentation of who you are. You will end up with what your flesh craved for, and end up losing who God created you for. "Eve," never confuse what God wanted you to go through with what you decided to deal with. You have to know when it's time to throw "Jonah's-disobedient-az" overboard and keep him off your ship! Sometimes a breakdown is necessary for a breakthrough, especially when it's time to breakup and breakout.

The man who is **allowed** to disrespect you is the man you're training to mistreat you. Thus, when the sound of a "demon alert" becomes distinctive, you have the right to assert a distasteful disposition. Why complain about the scorn if you allow it to become his norm? No ma'am, don't do that! Here is where I need to come out of the spirit and be real true to my ethnicity, or better yet, my Blackness. It's not a good look for attractive ladies to cuss, but if you have to come out of character a time or two, it may be cuss-worthy to give some "strong-az" voice instructions. "Going-in" and completely cussing a "nigga's-az" out will "nip some things in the bud."

Hey "Sis," I'm talking to you! After you breathe and decompress, remember that God offers "accident forgiveness!" Seriously, I was taught that if you accept a standard that is lower than what you were intended for, you will give death to the future that you were fitted for (LRL). Then again, when you have a clear understanding of your self-worth, you will feel empowered enough to **avoid** creating enabling environments for spoiled people whom you "pampered" at your own expense. Consistent with Keion Henderson: "You may have been **born** looking like your parents, but you **die** looking like your decisions." Don't decide to die because you were afraid to live!

Making people aware of my own limitations and the space that I should have taken ownership of, long ago, here is what I recently posted on Facebook: "If I am not on your payroll, I will not allow you to control which way, I 'roll'." People only react to you in the way that **you** train them to regard you. And usually, it's the people who are not paying that are the most demanding. As an "unsung hero" for many years, making this post was a polarizing moment for me. Because of doctoral achievements, it's time to demand the respect of a specialist and not a generalist! Thus, I made a conscious decision to stop allowing people to inconvenience **me** at **their** convenience. Since my time is valuable too, your return must match my reward. In other words, my self-worth is no longer up for negotiation! I will not continue to reduce myself so people can handle me.

Where was I before I went there? Inconsistently, what makes the cheating topic more poignant earlier is that my mom's husband had the audacity to confess to me that he had NEVER loved or cared for anyone else as much as he did the **disabled** woman. Absurdly (at 80 years old), he claimed that the most recent woman gave him the best sex that he had ever had. He had me "rolling." Nevertheless-also-even though," that's after my dear mom had given him FIVE-whole children. Maybe not "whole" in every sense of the word; yet, the sex couldn't have been that bad. Man of God, if you choose to stay stuck with her, make an effort to make the best of her, and not talk about her, to the rest of us. Now claiming that the most, recent wife used witchcraft on him, guess who has to feel the brunt of ALL his burdens?

In assuring me that he knows how to love and care for a woman, it pained my heart to hear him say that if he could love a physically-disabled woman who was also mentally-ill, surely he was capable of loving our mom. A powerful awareness stated by Oprah Winfrey is that, "If a man wants you, nothing can keep him away. If he doesn't want you, nothing can make him stay." Yet, his excuse was that our mom did not respect him as the man. So apart from the spirit of infidelity, what had been his real issue, all of these years? I agree with Steve Harvey who said: "You can't fix what's wrong with your home – outside your home." First and foremost, men respond to praise and have a need to be celebrated. At some point, my dad must have interpreted his wife and family as being individuals living in a group-home, as opposed to a family who respected and honored him, as the head **of** the home, **and** as the appreciated man in our lives.

Just as I had given so much attention and affection to other men who came into my life, I recently had an epiphany that may help to crack the man-code. Much of what my dad needed was for his family to validate who God called him to be (Reid, 2010). Even as respect should be earned, the sad and sobering reality is that some of his reactions may not have been wrong in theory. But in response, he was dead wrong; the least he owed my mother was a debt-of-honor.

Be that as it may, a valid point of view that resonates with me is this: until you understand that your man, by design, is a creature of ego and that you are summoned by the Creator to continuously stroke that ego, you are bound to have problems in the relationship. An ego-starved of praise will eventually begin to malfunction. Consequently, it will manifest as negligence, cheating, or even beating. According to my research, a man's ego is connected to his passion. Once you discover his passion, you should pour your praise into it. Some philosophies are flawed, and you cannot take them at face value, but this is one of those that must be considered. At any rate, it was always "the other woman" who fulfilled this need for my father.

Recently, when I refused to comply with his demands to control my decisions and treat me like a child, his agonizing, emotional abuse and verbal attacks were likely a result of an ego, starved of honor. Even in this case, I had to neutralize the power so that I could claim my weight as a 59 year-old woman, and not the irresponsible child that he wanted me to remain. In being his caretaker (by default), and often under his **wrath**, I completely empathize with what my mom suffered under his **watch**. If she was here to summarize her own experience, she would likely support this expression: "Marriage is like a deck of cards. In the beginning all you need is two hearts and a diamond. By the end, you wish you had a club and a spade" (Intimacy 4us's photo).

I absolutely love and respect the ministry of Iyanla Vanzant, but the one thing that I have to disagree on is that all women marry their fathers. Another reason that I may still be single is that I refuse to marry mine! Whatever the case may be, when two people claim to be born again, it seems that their spirits would dominate their bodies to make sure that their souls are at one. Question: With Adam and Eve having the divine nature of God, how did they allow sin to come in and dominate **their** world and wreak havoc on the rest of society? Firstly, woman, you must deal with the reality that you came out of the man. Just as man was created to be the HEAD, you must accept and consent to being the "neck" that supports the head. Manage your reality!

Adam had the authority, but when Eve's influence became stronger than the man's authority, the "neck" got out of place, and caused the body to be out of order. As a result of spiritual whiplash, the world has been out of order ever since, as it was the misalignment of the woman's power that caused the world to malfunction. Wow! It's just a fact: weak men help to debilitate incomplete-helpless women, but strong men help to validate whole-healthy women.

Secondly, Adam and Eve failed to act on what they knew, by not speaking to what they saw. If you really want to stay out of *divorce court* with someone you still have love for, speak the Word; prayer is on your side! It not only changes things; it changes people! If you change your **words**, you can use your voice-activated authority to change your **world**. You cannot go on "vocal rest" when your world depends on what you say. Rather than allowing damaging words to become your destructive reality, use your "voice command" to save your marriage.

Yes indeed, God is able to save your marriage because He honors marriage and hates divorce. Why does He hate divorce? Since the husband and wife represent Christ and the Church, divorce defeats God's purpose. Somewhere I learned that any representation of putting away (divorce) mars the picture that God wants to display. The word, divorce, means to tear; to be unattached after being joined. Also, divorce causes pain because the ripping apart of two people leaves permanent scars. Though the wound resulting from the tear may eventually heal, the scars of the tear remain visible through children, as a reminder of what was. Consequently, a child's shoulders were not built to bear the weight of their parents' choices. At the end of the day, "when you can look your kids in the face and say, 'I did everything I could to save the marriage,' only then have you earned the right to quit" (Dr. Phil).

Moses did not forbid divorce; yet, he had guidelines on how it should be done, likely to prevent the injustice from falling on the woman (Fenton, 2013). According to Jesus (Mt. 19:8), Moses permitted men to divorce their wives due to the hardness of a man's heart. If the husband did not provide food, clothing, and the duty of marriage, being the man's property, he had to free her. Thus, Moses provision of divorce was by reason of imperfect people marrying other people who were not perfect (Deu. 24:1-4).

The apostles record four instances in the Gospels where Christ addressed the issue of divorce: Matthew 5:31-32, Matthew 19:3-12, and Mark 10:2-12, and Luke 16:16. Please note Paul's discussion in 1 Corinthians 7:10-16. Even so, the questions on the floor are: What about God? Where does He stand on the topic of divorce? Since this court proceeding has gone way over the time, "Judge Ma-**bal**-lene" has called for a Recess to allow an opportunity for deliberation. Please take time to refresh, reenergize, and regroup, and we will meet you in the next chapter for further proceedings and closing arguments. This meeting is adjourned until you decide to return.

CHAPTER SIX

GOD – GUILTY OF DIVORCE

PART TWO OF "DIVORCE COURT"

"It seems to me that John 4:17 proves that God honors divorce OVER adultery. 'P☺W—W☺W!' Say with me: 'divorce OVER adultery.' If your marriage certificate certified that you were married to the **right** person, you wouldn't be trying to love more than one person at the SAME time." ☹
#K.DR

The recess has ended, and this "court" will come to order; we are ready to proceed. For those of you who are too "churchy" to know where I am going, allow me to explain the dichotomy of the chapter title. Here is where my research skills will take effect and go into full operation. Did you know that God was literally married to Israel? Yes, she was God's unfaithful wife for many centuries. Adultery was initiated within weeks of the marriage ceremony at Mount Horeb when she worshipped the golden calf (read the 32nd Chapter of Exo.).

The marriage continued during the time of the Judges and culminated in the days of Isaiah and Jeremiah. God, being *guilty of divorce*, we see that He divorced his wife in a lawful manner. He gave her a writ of divorce before sending her out of His house into the land of Assyria. Married for 726 years (from the marriage at Mount Horeb until the fall of Samaria), this was a divine example of both patience and forgiveness (Fenton, 2013).

Consistent with Fenton (2013), if divorce had been a sin, God would not have been able to divorce Israel, without committing a sin. We must conclude, then, that divorce is sometimes necessary, since many people over the centuries have found themselves in circumstances that were similar to what God has endured. We must also conclude that God shows consideration for divorce when there is the presence of sin (sexual immorality). In order to portray the unhappy marriage between God and Israel, Hosea, in particular, was called to marry a harlot. In Hosea 2:2 (KJV), he says: ***... "For she is not my wife, neither am I her husband."*** Also read Jeremiah 3:8.

In John 4:17, we see another textbook example. Jesus told the Samaritan woman who came to draw water, to go and call her husband, and then come back. She answered that she had no husband. Even though she had five husbands in the past, Jesus said to her, "You are correct to say that you have **no** husband. In fact, you have **had** five husbands, and the man you now have is not your husband." Technically, it sounds like this woman was shacking and had the nerve to come before the Judge. The crux of the matter is: since none of her five marriages were a "match made in heaven," Jesus agreed with her that she had no husband. Legally, she may have been married, but spiritually, she had no husband. It doesn't take God five times to get a perfect match.

I don't consider myself a Bible Scholar, but as an over-thinking-researcher, I should know how to at least, read between the lines. WHO society regards as your husband, may just be a relationship that God considers adultery. You may refuse to accept this concept because of your traditions that make God's Word of none effect. Even so, it seems to me that John 4:17 proves that God honors divorce OVER adultery. "P☺W—W☺W!" Say with me: "divorce OVER adultery." If your marriage certificate certified that you were married to the **right** person, you wouldn't be trying to love more than one person at the SAME time. ☹ Of course, when at all possible, we have **every** obligation to make the best out of our mess. But it can only happen when **both** parties agree to make it work. God can only operate when we agree to **coop**erate.

Even when the original Israelites were unfaithful to God and went after idols, those "Black" folks were just as we are today, stiff-necked, hardheaded, and uncircumcised in their heart and ears. Several times, God became so angry with them; He wanted to consume them. Ultimately, they found grace in His sight; and, to this day, He still considers "us" His chosen people. ***"Then will I remember My covenant with Jacob, and also My covenant with Isaac, and also My covenant with Abraham will I remember; and I will remember the land"*** (Lev. 26:42 KJV).

In ANY event, the marriage made at Mount Horeb between God and Israel was the Old Covenant. In this marriage contract or "conditional" covenant, God promised or vowed to bless and provide for Israel, and Israel vowed to obey God's laws. The covenant was broken and eventually came to an end because Israel was unable to fulfill her vow. That's when a New Covenant was needed; found in Jeremiah 31:31-33, it was a covenant that would endure. Unlike the Old Covenant, this covenant was based on the promise of God, rather than the obedience of man. Rather than depending on man's ability to fulfill their vows to God, the New Covenant depends on the ability of God to do as He has promised (Fenton, 2013).

It's the same as with salvation and deliverance; the Old Covenant was designed to fail from the beginning. However, the New Covenant was designed to succeed and make way for a better marriage. It is not by our ability and the limitations of our own human nature to fulfill our vows to God, but it's by God's ability to fulfill **His** vow. Even as the topic of salvation is always on point, but for the purposes and intents of this chapter, let me get back to the topic of divorce. If men and women were perfect, divorce would be unthinkable. So as God works His nature into us through the New Covenant, the possibility of divorce should become more and more remote, adds Fenton (2013).

So then, love may prolong a marriage, but it is your understanding of COVENANT that locks in the relationship. Thus, God continues to love Israel because of the **covenant** that He made with them. Some people I love, but I wouldn't dream of coming into a covenant agreement with. Contrary to popular belief, I even fell in love with folk that I would NOT want to be married to. Even though I was in, I still wanted out. Sometimes you fall in love by default, or because that was the only person who was willing to love you back. It is **not** so much that they were good enough to marry. The truth of the matter is: when you got your hands in the "lion's mouth," you get what you can until you can get what you need. And sometimes, you get what you don't want, until you can get your hands out and put them in the right mouth. That deserves a wink:,-)

Let's put my dad back on the "witness stand." Sometimes adult drama is simply, unresolved childhood trauma. As much as he dislikes me today, I must believe that much of his behavior is a result of a destructive pathology. As uneducated as he is/was, he understood that in the game of love, you must be **more than** a recipient. Even though he made for my mother, a "hot-bed-of-crazy," she still needed to make an effort to be a team player, a contributor, a participant – a giver, to attempt to make it work! In the event that he and my mother were opposites, the key to surviving was learning how to respect the agreement that you became a recipient of. To add to my racing thoughts, the understatement is that my parents were never created for one another. They got married without a true covenant. Real blessings bring joy and peace, not sorrow. ***"The blessing of the LORD, it maketh rich, and He addeth no sorrow with it"*** (Prov. 10:22 KJV).

Some blessings are counterfeit blessings – compliments of the devil himself! Stop lying to yourself that an abusive or negligent spouse is a blessing from God. Rather, humble yourself and admit that you simply **MISSED** God! Then, thank God that He is the God of a second chance. What my mother failed to act on is that you cannot lose yourself in the process of holding on to someone who does not care about losing you. You may need to go ahead and sign "them" papers.

Even though something good came out of a bad marriage (my sister and me), it was only because God promised us that ALL things would work together for the good. Lost in the discussion, did I forget to mention that there were older brothers that came out of this union? The oldest sibling, who has never been accused of being the "sharpest tool in the shed," and the other brother; well, I'm either lost for words for once, or just too exhausted to dig him up. #hot-to-the-mess.com! ((({..})) #Headaches&More is the name of my family tree.

Arriving at the essence of this family experience, those guys just reminded me to make another significant point. The genetic aspect to this is that you need to look at the family tree and make sure that you are not marrying into a full-blown curse. When folks are not supposed to be married, they create children who never should have been born (or who would have been better off staying where they were). But the point is: when you don't know what demons a family is fighting, you take a chance on linking your children into a system of DYSFUNCTION! Even as there are inherited, **familiar** spirits, we simply need to be more discerning about what comes into our **families. Can you** see the connection between those, two words? Particularly when children are involved, a covenant is not godly unless **God is involved**!

Since there was no chance of this relationship ever working out, would my mother have been better off divorcing him, way before my father decided to make his exit, permanent? They tried several times to reconcile, and there was a time when they even renewed their vows. Eventually, after my he had committed serial adultery, God finally gave my mom a legal-spiritual, "cut-off-notice." Either you love your home enough to stay and pray; or, you value your soul enough to run and take refuge. Allow me to say it another way: don't chase it; allow God to replace it!

Inseparable from its meaning, my mother chose to keep getting extensions that apparently contributed to her expiration. Even on her death bed, she made reference, yet again, to the most recent situation that had made her feel neglected in the worst way. You never have to forgive anyone that you don't blame. So since she blamed him, she needed to forgive him, and she wanted him to forgive her. Otherwise, if she had not cared, she would have left in silence. It's the people that you love that will make you put up a fight. As she was still coherent, I made sure that she not only released my father from that situation. I ushered her into demolishing any old "bridges" that could prevent her from taking the right "highway" to her new home.

While my dad was offended that she would not allow him to feed her during those final days, the last thing that I facilitated before she completely became incoherent was a phone call to apologize. Oddly enough, he still remembers to bring it up, but the sad reality of dementia is that it does not allow him to remember her apology. Now, he expects me to treat him like a king, after he abandoned my mother and treated her like a peasant. Often at the brunt of his wrath, the only request I deny him is to allow him to live with me. But do you understand why I "go hard" at giving him the **best** of care (making sure his meds are taken accurately, doctors' visits made when necessary, bills paid on time, hot meals served, etc)?

It's not so much that I'm so kind (which I am), or what's in it for me at the end of his life. Side-note: even with total access to his assets, I refuse to mishandle what's already mine. To steal from him would be to steal from myself. The crux of the matter is that I go the extra mile because God has given me a clean heart and renewed in me, the right spirit. Besides Luke 6:27-28, I am also obeying Ephesians 6:2-3 (KJV): ***"Honor your father and mother... that it may be well with thee, and thou mayest live long on the earth."*** The last conversation that I had with the late Mother Ida M. Porter, she felt led to tell me that THIS is why I'm blessed. She even felt that God may have extended my life, so that I could still be here to take care of my dad.

Although my parents never made it to divorce court, this series of events was the consequence of two people who were never taught that since God was guilty of divorce Himself, he honors divorce **over** adultery. In terms of social meanings and implications, as well as personal and professional values, we are aware that stress is a known killer. While I have had eight, MAJOR surgeries for abdominal adhesions and one for breast cancer, along with systemic lupus, and life-threatening blood clots, I can attest to the fact that pain has a way of twisting itself inside. So much so, that during one of my surgeries, the doctor indicated that my intestinal organs were so twisted and matted together that it looked like someone had melted them in saran wrap.

Since hurts often turn into "knots," would it be a fallacy to say that the stress from a bad marriage was indeed a significant factor in my mother's death? With what you have witnessed in Part Two of "divorce court," do you really think that it was God's perfect will for my saintly mother to remain married to someone who was unwilling to support her, financially? Was it God's will for my mom (a praying woman who loved Him with every fiber of her being), to live a painful/miserable life and die with a broken heart and a tattered and torn body? Literal tears here, but I think **not**!

Could the man's soul be corrupt because his rib is connected to the wrong woman? Likewise, since the rib protects the heart and lungs, could her heart be aching because of the bone that has been dislocated? Sometimes when walking away FROM, what you cannot pray yourself out OF, the most radical disconnection may become your greatest deliverance! That was #tweetable! At the point that a relationship shifts to "no-return," just REPOSITION, and refrain from allowing that person to come back into your "inner court." Continue to walk in love, but protect your heart by keeping your boundaries and establishing limitations. Taken as a whole, if your marriage is broken, fix it! If it CAN'T be fixed, replace it! The abusive spouse that REFUSES to change is broken beyond repair. Get a new one! Only a fool keeps what another fool refuses to fix.

Your heavenly Father loves you far more than your earthly father. Now if your earthly father would not want you to remain in an abusive marriage, how could you possibly believe that your loving, heavenly Father would want you to remain in an abusive marriage? God didn't sit there and rejoice at the day of your birth, only to see you grow up to marry an idiot! Even as God says He hates divorce (Mal. 2:16); He hates the **act of** divorce, not the **need for** divorce.

In other words, God does not hate the act of an abused spouse divorcing his/her abusive spouse. He hates the fact that persistent, unrepentant, abusive behavior inevitably leads to the necessity of divorce, when all the abusive spouse had to do was stop being abusive. God never desires an *abusee* to remain with an abuser! If your spouse is abusing you, don't call the pastor for prayer or the police to make peace; you need to call **"Two Men & A Truck,"** and get the hell out! "Coming home in a failed marriage is better than coming home in a coffin" (Athena).

Please do not misinterpret my message; God really does hate divorce, particularly, if a couple is just too lazy to salvage a sanctioned marriage. According to Drk DMeggett, "One reason marriages (even those ordained by Abba) don't work is because we don't do the work before we say, 'I do.' #get healed." Again, what God ordains, He's obligated to sustain. However, in the event that He had absolutely nothing to do with your marriage, the positive spin on divorce is that it is a mistake that **can be** excused. Therefore, I am not supporting daunting divorces, but I **am** promoting respectable relationships!

I am aware that some denominations have strict rules regarding divorce, but who cares what they think or how they feel, when God has the right to tell you what He needs you to know. I am in agreement with the notion that institutional betrayal occurs when performance or reputation is valued over the well-being of members. Specifically, pressuring members to maintain the ILLUSION of a healthy marriage, even when domestic violence is occurring is normalizing abuse! I am here to interrupt the pattern and challenge the system that should be designed to defend, respond, protect, and seek justice for the victim.

While the Church's emphasis is on "maintaining appearance" at all costs, even parallels have been drawn between hiding incest within families and covering up abuse within organizations. When remained unchecked, what role has your church or community played in the development of a person's destructive pathology when it chooses either, not to respond, or place blame at the feet of the traumatized victim?

Above and beyond, how can the church teach that everything else is under the blood and treat divorce as an unpardonable act against God? As this is an unwarranted deception, the deception merits my next question: Are we really walking in the spirit of atonement; or, are we just operating out of an awareness of the painful outcome of our bad decisions? Even while some people pass judgment on other folks' second marriage, their first and only marriage is no indication that they have the **perfect** marriage! Wow! I just sent my own-self a Cash App. L☺L!

Logical in his assertion, Dr. R. A. Vernon asks: "What good is having a mega church and a storefront marriage?" As well, Pastor, "don't expect [First Lady] to play her part when you've got other people auditioning for her role!" (Baisden Live). Now that was for Pastor; here is my question to the prophet: How can you be a prophet to the nations and not be a papa to your children. You are a "whole" "Dead-beat-az!" Go somewhere and SAT down somewhere!,-)

Does God really expect us to become so connected to the dead-weight of these "dead-beats" that they disconnect us from our destiny? In contradiction to your tradition, how can you be true to God if you are living under false pretenses and not being true to yourself? How can you logically counsel other folks whose marriages are "jack'd" up, while your fantasies are driven by someone else? If I had to make a choice, I would much rather be divorced from my mistake than to be disconnected from my mandate. For reasons previously noted: why justify being miserable in a "situation-ship," when marrying **right** will complete your life? On the other hand, why rationalize the tolerance of a hell-mate, when a divorce justifies you to be your own bedmate?

Thank you for listening to my philosophies and borrowed theories; now back to what I want to conclude from my research. When Adam and Eve were first created, their marriage was initially patterned after the New Covenant, just as they **knew** the will of God and were obedient to Him by nature. Before they sinned, they served each other, equally. It was **after** they sinned that God knew that disagreements among married couples would occur. It was at that point that He had to initiate authority, as in Genesis 3:16. In my "must-read," *Hey Adam, Where You At?* I draw some very interesting parallels and cover many intriguing aspects as related to this topic.

Once we understand how things changed after Adam and Eve sinned, we can understand Jesus' words in Matthew 19, where He stressed the New Covenant's unity and agreement between husband and wife. Meanwhile, since we still live in an imperfect world that is incorporated with sin, the law is yet needed to keep order. It is also needed to teach us what God intends to write on our hearts so that we may be conformed to the image that He intended from the beginning. When Moses allowed divorced, Jesus did not put away this law. Rather, He told us to go <u>beyond</u> Old

Covenant marriage into perfect unity, where divorce is unnecessary and irrelevant (Fenton, 2013).

Where leaders are concerned, I feel compelled to add some biblical insight from Pastor Larry Stockstill (2014), particularly since the bishops were not addressed earlier. Perhaps, this may lead to a slightly different conclusion. "The Scripture qualifies a leader as the 'husband of one wife' (1 Tim. 3:2). A leader who 'unscripturally' divorces (that is, divorces for any reason other than spousal adultery), or whose spouse divorces him should step down from ministry for an extended period in the hope of restoring his or her marriage. The leader must not consider remarriage to a different partner until his spouse has remarried and reconciliation therefore becomes impossible. All initial efforts must be toward restoration of their home, not beginning a new life with someone else."

While I dare not "fudge" on this scriptural interpretation, the same, basic adage applies for leaders alike: "Loving someone who doesn't love you is like waiting for a **ship** at the **air**port" (origin unknown). And since you know that you will not find a ship at the airport, God deals with our mistakes to a moral expectation of fairness. Consequently, "we suffer diminished access to accuracy and richness when parts of the human family are silenced, ignored, exploited, or oppressed" (Sommers-Flanagan & Sommers-Flanagan, 2007).

Just as my discussion of divorce is totally based around infidelity, abuse and neglect, I must cover all of my bases if you are contemplating divorce for any other reason. Here I advise you to take Dr. Phil's Divorce Readiness Test to ascertain if you are really **ready** for divorce. Check it out at: www.drphil.com/advice/calling-it-quits-are-you-ready-for-divorce/. As long as rule #1 is to never be #2, it is likely that you may simply need to go to a "Marriage Boot-Camp" and learn to appreciate what you have before it becomes what you had. Rather than ending up in *divorce court*, you may discover that you are far better off with what you have than what you think you want (wink,-). Don't be greedy when it's time to be grateful!

In the event that you choose to go to a type of "Marriage Boot-Camp," here are some valid nuggets to share with the group. "Because a woman is a creature of emotion, her number one need is a sense of security. To give her this sense of security, multiple times a day you should hold her, caress her, massage her, or touch her with your hands in some non-sexual way. Alternatively, because a man is a creature of ego, his number one need is praise! And it is your responsibility, woman of God, to stroke his ego through praise. A man's ego is connected to his passion. Wherefore, you must first discover what your man's number one passion is in life; then, you must praise him every day in relation to that passion. This will make him feel like you are the most wonderful woman on earth," says Prophet Floyd Barber. "Now 'Eve,' 'where **you** at'?"

Here, I am reminded of an occasion that is relative to this conclusion. One of my friends, who had been married for 30 years, was extremely perturbed that her husband had planned a root canal on the day that she was scheduled for breast cancer surgery. In the heat of the moment, she paused and said to me: "I know you want a man, but just stay with Jesus" (☺). I wanted to giggle out loud, but in trying to deescalate a very delicate situation, I told her to charge it to the last generation. Maybe the men in his life never taught him how to be sensitive to a woman's needs. On the whole, some men are even experiencing arrested development.

In my attempt to prevent her from emasculating him, even her son commented that I was trying hard to find some good in all the bad. Yet, she did not let the day of surgery end without sharply expressing her feelings. My case in point: a docile and unassuming man cannot be at peace with a strong, Black woman. In arriving at this position, also consider this strand in the fabric of marriage: ***... "And the wife see that she reverence her husband"*** (Eph. 5:33b KJV)**.** In learning how to apply our mouths better than we apply our make-up, Proverbs 15:1 KJV (with emphasis added) must become applicable: ***"A SOFT answer turneth away wrath: but grievous words stir up anger."***

As for me, I did not expect to still be single and a couple of weeks from turning 60; however, divorce is just not an option. Such as the nature of the New Covenant, if both husband and wife choose to live in accordance to the will of God and allow His character and the mind of Christ to be infused into their hearts, there should be no need for divorce. Until I can come into such an agreement with whomever he may be, *Boaz or "No-az,"* I will continue to WAIT on purpose. **OR**, I will continue to FULFILL my purpose. Either way, I hope that the following quote will capture the feeling of most singles: "Single is not a status. It is a word that best describes a person who is strong enough to live and enjoy life without depending on others. Someday, you will be the best thing that ever happened to someone... Until then: become the best thing that ever happened to YOURSELF" (Facebook status). "Divorce Court" is finally adjourned.

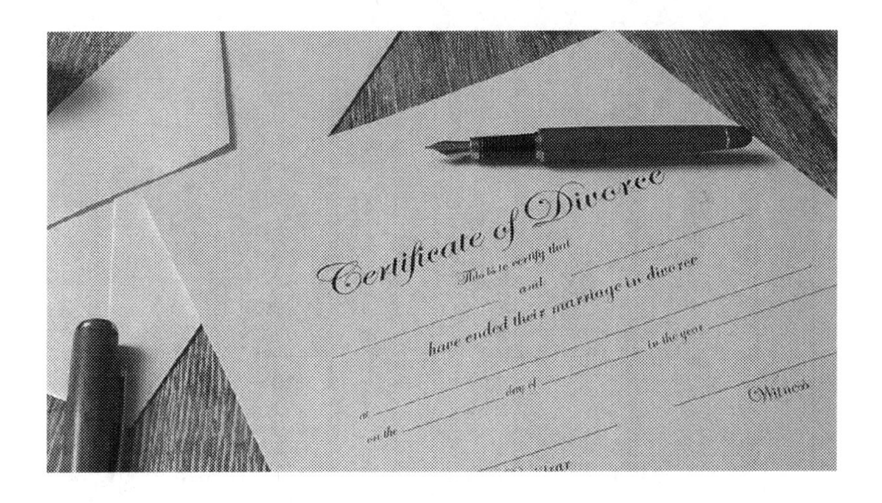

CHAPTER SEVEN

"FALSE ALARMS"

"No matter how much a man desires you, you must make sure that he really **deserves** you? When asked by a prayer warrior if I thought that he could cover me, my response: 'SORRY,'
YOU ARE NOT THE ONE!
Prayer was not created to pay bills; **work** was. I need a man with both a prayer ministry **AND** an employment history!" #K.DR

After coming out of a 15-year emotionally, abusive relationship, I really hate to call my first dating experience a *false alarm.* He was more like an "angel" that God had sent into my life to protect me, as I was trying to find my way in a small, military town, where I often went to visit my family and work as a vendor. He wasn't just a "fly-by-nighter" either; he became a "Full-Bird" Colonel in the Army, with the capacity to become a General. Now that's powerful! He had such an intense desire to cover me, without ever imposing upon the established goals and plans that were already in motion. From a plaque, I eventually understood the reality of angels; it went like this: "Friends who take time to care are really angels unaware."

Taking me under his "angel wings," he understood his divine assignment and was totally considerate of my agenda. That blessed me! Out of all the single soldiers on this particular base, who desired to take me out on a date, this was definitely, a godly-connection. "I know you were a very special person the moment I met you. You were not an average lady who just wanted to flaunt your beauty. Instead, you were naturally forthcoming, impressive, and unshakable in your sales presentation – 'Either you want it or you don't.' Through your book, I learned to let go and forgive those who have trespassed against me, and never to hold bad feelings against those who have mistreated me, in spite of broken trust. Your book touches the moral fabric of our lives and gives us new meaning about what it takes to be a survivor"…

By nature, we demonstrated many of the same, spiritual fruit. So what was my dilemma? He "winged it" like the perfect angel, but where I was expecting God to take me, I needed someone who was **spiritually-**balanced, and rooted and grounded in what I believe. God can only trust people with me who have evolved in the things of Him. In order to choose the man that is suitable for the Anointing that God has released onto my life, I "gotta" go spiritual. I must seek involvement based on who I know **I** am, rather than settling for who I am hoping **he becomes.** By doing so, I cannot allow my flesh to select "the most-eligible bachelor." Why not? The most eligible-naturally may not be the most-compatible, spiritually. When you deal with folks you want to live with for life, you must not only make a physical connection. Your association must dictate a marked, spiritual-attraction that will permanently create a striking, natural affection (Reid, 2010).

At any rate, it is not necessary that my future husband and I have the same denominational history, but our spiritual destinies should interrelate in some way that it gives us a firm foundation. My marriage will not dictate my ministry; rather, my marriage <u>must</u> synchronize **with** my ministry. Precisely, my ministry cannot be contaminated by a complicated marriage. A loosed woman deserves a loosed man. Otherwise, I may have been the next Mrs. "Colonel J..." One of the most gentle and affirming men that I have ever met, we are still friends today.

I told my comedic, pastor-friend, that I could have easily held on to the "wings" of my "angel-friend," had we been spiritually-compatible. He replied: ... "And you have known him for six months? By now, he should be speaking in tongues **and** operating in <u>three</u> gifts. J I even wrecked the Colonel's beautiful, new truck. He repaired it and continued to soar with me on the wings of pure, untainted friendship. So what was my dilemma? Since I am so "out-of-this-world" myself, my special task was to keep him from singing, "You are the wind beneath my wings."

My military "angel" touched my heart in so many ways, while consistently emphasizing that I was very low-maintenance and far too easy to please. For instance, whenever I received a call on my cell phone, he politely stepped aside to allow me the privacy I needed to handle my business. Little things like that meant so much, coming out of "protective custody." Even if "Uncle Sam" helped to influence his exceptional etiquette and matchless manners; either way, the well-bred soldier knew how to treat a lady. Whoever came after the Colonel had quite an act to follow.

While in Hawaii, as my most profound friend, Damaras (Renee) and I were discussing whether the Colonel was "da-one," I took note of her reflective wisdom. "You can know what's right for you, but have an attraction for what's familiar to you. The 'it' factor could be blocking your vision for who God has for you." I recall Bishop D. Dewayne Rudd making a similar point: "You can be blinded to what you need because you are addicted to what you want." Both points may have been worth considering, but years later and learning to saying yes to God has taught me when to say no to man. The Colonel and I have both moved on, and I believe that I am right now, where God knew I would be. *Why DIDN'T I Get Married?* You know the answer!

While working at the airport shortly afterwards, a concerned co-worker, called me at my gate and said, "Code Red-Code Red!" I was like, "What girl? Is there a fire or something?" She responded, "No, it's a good-looking 'red-bone,' dressed in black, coming your way." L☺L! Hilariously, I responded: "Code Red-Code Red, please meet Code Brown at Gate A1." With passengers staring me in the face, I became so tickled that I could hardly keep my composure.

Another time Angela called and summoned me to her gate, she said, "Come quick; your husband is at my gate. He is a **CAPTAIN,** and he is pleasant to the eye." After securing my flight and literally rushing to her gate, my "so-called husband" was ironically the last passenger to board her aircraft. Indiscreetly, I asked, "Sir, who do you fly for?" Surprisingly, he was a pastor of two churches, and was on his way to preach. Another *false alarm* in the gate area, A.J. had misrepresented the man's profile. To resolve the confusion, she then claimed, "Oh, he is a 'Captain' for Jesus. That makes it even better." Her humor was over the top, crazy and contagious. I ended up going out a couple of times with one, other pastor who had come through my gate. After "rapid testing," he tested positive for another *false alarm.* #FondAirportMemories

Later I met a very spiritual brother whose day revolved around praying, sleeping, eating, and talking on the phone. Over $50,000 behind in child support, I couldn't even **PAY** this prayer warrior to wash my car! While my dear friend was categorically a *false* alarm, this review is not intended to be criticism; it's an observation. The wife that he ended up with justified his laziness (I meant lifestyle) by saying that sometimes you have to accept the packaging that the gift comes wrapped in. Judge Lynn Toler says it best: "You can't marry 'Hope;' you 'gotta' marry a Man!"

As he was simply good company and someone I enjoyed hanging out with, he eventually claimed that God said, I was his wife. It was then that I started preaching my greatest "sermons." When God spoke to the man, He gave him a command. **Before** He gave Adam permission to eat of the tree, He first took the man and put him in the Garden of Eden to dress it (Gen. 2:15- 16). He watched and prayed, while he worked. The Garden was designed to give man a **job**, not a retreat. He was to work it and to keep it (shamar means to protect it). Clearly, God was circumventing the proclivity of man becoming lazy, as in Proverbs 13:4 (NLT).

Even in Paradise, before the pleasure of eating came the task of **working**. Also, Jacob was willing to **work** 14 years for Rachael before he was able to claim her. Real love will make you **work** for what you want. That's what it means for the man to take DO-MIN-ION (MEN DO). Likewise, before Jesus chose the disciples, they were already working. Any man who's looking for an excuse **not** to work is unquestionably, a *false alarm.* #TotallyUnacceptable!

Don't force me to go to work, just because I got with you! If a woman is coming with the ability to help you, she is a type of Paraclete, who must be given honor by her head, just as the Holy Spirit gives honor to Jesus Christ. The point is: you must already be doing something! The Woman's #1 Christian Radio Stations are: W.Y.W.W. "**W**hat **Y**ou **W**orking **W**ith," and W.I.F.M. "**W**hat's **I**n **I**t **F**or **M**e?" If you are unwilling to work to care for me once you connect with me, you won't be able to hold me, honor me, or hang on to me, once you marry me! "Hey 'Adam,' 'where you at'?" Did you not know that the Word teaches us not to have company with a man who is too lazy to work? Watch this...

"For even when we were with you, this we commanded you, that if any would not work, neither should he eat. For we hear that there are some which walk among you disorderly, working not at all, but are busybodies. Now them that are such we command and exhort by our Lord Jesus Christ, that with quietness they work, and eat their own bread. But ye, brethren, be not weary in well doing. And if any man obey not our word by this epistle, note that man, and have no company with him, that he may be ashamed" (2 Thes. 3:10-14 KJV).

Quite the reverse, Ecclesiastes 5:12a (KJV) reveals: ***"The sleep of a labouring man is sweet"...*** Make no mistake about it; work was not given to harm you! It is God's method of helping you to provide **and** leave an inheritance for your family. When a man dies without life insurance, which is one of the main reasons why he should have taken his lazy behind to work, the widow has to depend on family and church folks to scramble up money, just to send him back to the dirt. In the casket, it looks as though he's peacefully looking up at you and saying, "Thanks 'y'all' for 'footing' my six-foot bill." A "trifling-az," even in the casket! L☺L!

Since God does things decently and in order (1 Cor. 14:40), it does not matter how well a man can preach, pray or prophesy, if his gift does not afford him health and life insurance, he needs to go out and find a JOB. "Man of God, WE ARE NOT HERE TO ENABLE YOU, OR MAKE UP FOR YOUR MANHOOD because you believe that the Anointing on your life is bigger than a 9 to 5!" As this is a last-minute rant and some "drive-by" edits, are you still wondering *why I didn't get married*? #Novices-in-the-Pulpit is another good reason!

The advantage of having a husband is that you get at least, three benefits: a priest, a **PROVIDER**, and a protector. Once you come into the picture, it is not about where I'm going; the question becomes: Where are **you** taking me? If you do not have a 401(k) plan, you must not plan to take me far. And surely, if you do not have a job, you likely don't have a 401(k) plan! Why should I let you "sweat" **on** me, if you can't "sweat" **for** me? Here was the unexpected element about this last *false alarm*. He had the nerve to ask me if I **thought** that he could cover me? Wrong question; he set himself up for some more Gospel truths!

Well, after I had been a plus to his life for a good while, he finally came into some money from a settlement. Out of curiosity and to solicit a response to see where his heart was, I asked if he would simply buy me a meal. Guess what happened. Driving a car on a suspended license that someone else had signed for, he brought me some leftovers from a meal that he had bought himself. "I was D☹NE!" A man with a self-absorbed mentality would **never** be capable of covering a woman with a philanthropic mindset. No matter how much a man desires you, you must make sure that he really **deserves** you? Without a "pot to piss in, or a window to throw it out," I informed him that the **ONLY** way he could cover me was in prayer! Nevertheless, prayer without principles equals a "broke-az-prophet" without progression. #Limited&Local Besides, God would not expect me to submit to a man who refuses to work. :-/

I even moved him into my home for a short time, to allow him to start a part-time job and become more independent. Not long after he finally started working, he got injured, regressed back to his comfort zone, and moved back home. "Where they do 'dat' at?" Prayer was not created to pay bills; **work** was. I need a man with both a prayer ministry AND an employment history! Every month, I would hate to depend on getting a prayer through when my rent was due. Since I am not marrying the **name** of Jesus (rather in Jesus' name), I expect to take my husband's name to the bank. According to Exodus 21:21, a sign of immaturity and instability is a man that lives from hand to mouth because he is equivalent of his money.

You cannot effectively defend a woman without any money. Exodus 21:10 suggests that my lifestyle should not diminish when I take on my husband's name. The name of Jesus will heal all of my diseases, but when I say my husband's name at the mortgage company, I expect the keys to the house. When I use his social security number at the car dealership, I should be able to walk away with the "**Bentley**." Now, let me reverse the question for this same friend who tenaciously fought **and** prayed to get his disability started: Do **YOU** think that you could have covered me?

Sickly ever after, maybe his wife needed a male, but I want a man that needs me. # P☺W! A real man knows that if he does not work, he cannot eat! He also understands the adage, that the only place success comes before work is in the dictionary. Before Eve showed up, Adam was not trying to figure out a way to talk, think, agree and believe himself into a legitimate condition of disability, so that he could minister to the animals and avoid keeping the Garden. Likely still working multiple jobs and conditioned to participate in his fulltime, disability ministry, my friend's wife probably realizes more and more that she was probably doing bad, better by herself.

Along these lines: "As a man thinketh," what? … ***"Poverty and shame shall be to him that refuseth instruction" …*** (Prov. 13:18 KJV). It's too late in the game to deal with a novice. By now, the man who chooses to cover me should own a home that I can be proud to live in, a car that I am not ashamed to be seen in, a checking account that we can count on, and at least, a savings account that we can live off, in cases of an emergency. Otherwise, I will continue to do **better** by myself! To be single is not only a lifestyle; for me it has become my ministry!

In the process of turning off the *false alarm* and preaching to my friend until I was "blue in the face," I almost destroyed a friendship because I did not appropriately handle his ego. If you are seeking to crack your "man-code," you should seriously take this advice into consideration. ***… "In quietness and in confidence shall be your strength" …*** (Isa. 30:15b KJV). Even as I am naturally quiet, this was the one person who could make me "preach without a manuscript." ☺ As it was my intention to provoke him to perfection, I concluded that in order to upgrade my communication skills, I must be able to give-in whenever I feel the compulsion to out-talk.

I must commit to memory that "even the ornament of a meek and quiet spirit is in the sight of God of great price" (1 Pet. 3:4). As well, when it comes to issues regarding a man's ego and leadership role, ladies, we must encase **unsolicited** ideas in the form of a query, rather than in the form of an argument. If not, he may become defensive and refuse to consider your wisdom as a form of **constructive** criticism.

At any rate, when you are a Proverbs 31 woman, particularly by the age of 50-60 years old, your struggling days should be over. Nobody should be able to use you as a "come-up." Yes, it is part of my duty to help continue building my husband up; however, I am coming to water that, which was **ALREADY** planted. In other words, my planting season is over; it's harvest time now! I don't mind maybe, "**RE**paving the driveway," but I am not trying to build a whole, new "sidewalk." Since iron sharpens iron, and a man sharpeneth the countenance of his friend, relationships are designed to make you better – not worse.

COMPATIBILITY VS. COMPROMISE: Do you want compatibility, or are you so desperate that you are willing to compromise your standard of excellence for a *false alarm*? If you cannot go to the doctor under his insurance, or at least have your teeth cleaned under his benefits, he is a *false alarm* (a novice). And, if **both** of your credit reports are "jack'd" up, and together you can't even qualify for your FIRST home, not to mention a HUD home, you are not going to start off with a fresh marriage. What you will do is complicate your consistent ability to provide him with "*fresh flesh* [intimacy] *and flickering flames* [romance]" Again, *Why Didn't I Get Married? Boaz Or "No-az." I'm Waiting On Purpose.*

Personally, if you are not helping me, you must be hurting me. There has to be a point when a male stops being one of the boys and he becomes a man who makes deposits rather than withdrawals! I like Wonder Wombman's difference between a BOY and a MAN: B. O. Y. (Burden On You)... M. A. N. (Meets All Needs). A male simply cannot capitalize on his masculinity without maximizing his manhood. Consequently, if your "Boo" is not fit to be a king, you may need to become his deliverer. In order to be a deliverer, you need to first, HEAL the head – not "SCREW" the head.

As Joyce Meyer teaches, to win a battle, you must start with the mind. God did not birth David to **remain** a shepherd; He prepared him to be somebody's king. He had to mature in his mentality. When you become a king, you must be clever enough to oversee your own battles. You cannot send other men out to fight for you so that you can relax on a roof and lust after another man's wife. And then, because of irrational thinking, you have her husband killed. When you are in a king's posture, gross lapses in judgment will make you choose lust over logic.

In due time, I will get back to revealing my *false alarms,* but allow me to teach. Ecclesiastes 10:16 suggests that woe comes to those whose king is a child (also read verses 17-20). If God has not yet manifested your king, there is a strong possibility that he is still in a growing process. Be patient; kings are not born; they must be processed and developed over time. God does not want to give you anyone that is ill-prepared for battle. When your king is a child, you may or may not have utilities. You may have a car to drive, or you may not. You may have housing this month and be in a shelter next month. You may get kissed today and slapped the next.

The highest honor a man can give a woman is to wait on love/marriage to have sex. Either way, if you are having sex with a *false alarm*, the "Cussing Pastor" calls it, "poverty-penis." You may have reacted to this reference with skepticism, but it's when a woman has to pick up the man because he has no car. She has to pump the gas because he is disabled. She has to purchase the home in her name because he has no credit. With no etiquette at the restaurant, he is so ignorant that he tells you to get an entry because he doesn't know what an entree is. According to Thaddeus, if a man is that broke, he needs to go on a "penis diet." #Meat-free

As flawed as it may sound, the sign of a "poverty-penis" is when a "grown-az" man does not have a car and is still living at home with his mama. In the "Cussing Pastor's" exact words, "a king without a kingdom 'ain't' shit." He suggests that if he is not working, he needs to take the "matter" into his own hands, and "jack-off" and stop slanging that "poverty-penis" around. I apologize for the cultural words of expression, but that was "one for the books."

Now, let me not be biased here. What are some indications that your queen is still a teen? If she packs her bags and run home to mama every time that you bring correction or instruction, you may have married a girl.

You may get a half-cooked meal one day, and some McDonalds the next. You may get some sex this week, and she may have the cramps for the next six months. Again, when you find a real wife, Proverbs 18:22 assures that you shall find "good" because of the favor of God that is upon her life. In my book, **anything other than favor is *false*!**

I met my next *false alarm* at a Leadership Conference in 2013. A few weeks later, around Valentine's Day, I received a card in the mail with three, crisp 100 dollar bills. Money talks, and it will convince you to talk back. L☺L! So after a few, captivating telephone conversations and an intriguing lure to become the "First Lady" of his ministry, I thought that MAYBE, I could make this work. He did not really "wow" me, but at least he seemed to have been a good "possible-potential" and someone that could grow **on** me.

Feeling the phone conversations more than I was feeling the actual chemistry, by Valentine's Day, I was singing, "Amazing Love." By the next Valentine's Day, I was back to singing, "Amazing Grace!" LJL Those who rush in always rush out! I may have been fascinated by the idea, but I was NOT in love with the reality. Needless to say, I declined on *purpose* and made the choice to say: "Yo-az" is positively, not my Boaz!" This *false alarm* had some baggage that was better lost than found. "Y'all," I'm enjoying my own "c☺☺king!"

Can I go ahead and be transparent, right here? He presented himself as an apostle with a devoted prayer life, but when the *alarm* went off, he turned out to be, not only a "lying-az" but also a "drinking-az." How incongruent was that? Incongruence is when your behavior does not line up with who you say you are. Even as I come with my own, heavy baggage, at the end of the day, we must unite with people who care enough to help us unpack. As I was very open and transparent, he knew up front what he was dealing with. As he was willing to help me unpack my baggage, the Spirit had to REVEAL his baggage to me. If I had not been sharp and discerning, I could have ended up with some surprises and habits that I was not willing to accept or support.

Yes, he was willing to spend money on me, but even as I have never been a "gold-digger," it was not the same as having a man to invest in me. Know the difference. Consequently, I found out on the **first** visit, everything that I needed to know to make a quality decision. My brother-Bishop

Porter gave us a quick, "pre-dated" counseling session after service that Sunday. And because he did not want me to end up with another *false* alarm, he went as far as allowing the apostle to preach in his pulpit that night. Jokingly, I told him recently: "You'll allow **any**body to preach in your pulpit." But that time, he was trying to find out if this guy was a user or a loser.

By the third day, I was ready to send the brother on an "Uber ride" to "Never-never-land!" Without a doubt, I had not met my Boaz and had awakened the "wrong-az." No, I think I woke up a "praying-inebriated-az." When I first picked him up from the airport, it was obvious that he'd had more than a **little** wine on the plane. Extremely hyped, giddy and jittery, that brother had been drinking since the night before. And then, he lied and said that he had been taking pain pills, when the scent of alcohol was oozing from his pores. By experience, pain pills calm you all the way down, "Boo." They do not pump you all the way up. At any rate, this was a bonafide *false alarm.* "Adam," go back to sleep, and do not wake up until you're sober and DELIVERED!

I just received a phone call from a long-standing acquaintance, who maintains that even though I have admitted to him that my heart is somewhere else, I still have a spell on him. He insists that I am beautiful and smart, but it is my spirit that is so inviting, and that makes him willing to fight for me. He even texted me a copy of his payroll check to prove that he is well-capable of providing for me. If he really knew my taste, he would have had second thoughts about texting me his check stub. I have been dreaming of, and looking at million-dollar mansions for the past 15 years. I feel like the man of God who said to Amaziah, in 2 Chronicles 25:9b (KJV): ***"The LORD is able to give thee much more than this."***

Now don't get me wrong, this dude would make some lady a "dang-good" husband. He's handsome; he works hard, and most of all, he loves God. In 2016, in a moment of desperation (technically homeless and ready for some help), I texted him to see if he would be willing to relocate to Dallas. Accordingly, he was willing to transfer his job, **and** build me a home twice the size that he had recently built for himself. "Ladies, don't ever let what a man bring to the table be all you have to eat" (Codelblack Comedy's Photo). As I had always considered him to be like a brother (with no romantic chemistry), God went ahead and made some changes in my life to keep me from even considering, surrendering to a (reasonable) *false alarm*.

Where there was no true connection, there would have been no real covenant. And where there is no true covenant, there is no full-covering. You can't be covered and not be connected. And I don't ever want to be in covenant with anybody that cannot cover me completely. If you see my nakedness, I need to know that you can cover me? I need to know I can still feel you, even when I can't see you, or you can't see me. Even if I can't touch your body, I need to be sure that I can still smell your presence. Although my friend has consistently tried to convince me (for years) that he could love me more than any other man, love or money cannot keep you married. Again, it is your understanding of COVENANT, and that it goes far beyond the certificate.

Finally, my most recent dating experience was more of a friend than a *false alarm*. I often think of him as my crisis manager. I don't believe that God could have sent me a better friend than that of "Mr. G." And since he has spent the most time with me than any other man has in the past, nine years, I will devote this next section to him. I enjoy hanging out with him because I enjoy his sense of humor. Not only is he witty and clever, he can cook his butt off! Right now, I owe about 15 of my pounds to "Mr. G.'s" cooking.

He is simply a respectable man who will go out of his way to do whatever I need him to do. And since he thinks that I am his personal assistant, I feel that the exchanges have been equally-rewarding. Recently, after royally celebrating me for my 60th birthday, he said to me as I was getting out of the car, "I'll talk to you later, with 'yo' good-letter writing ass." "I hollered!" I often confer with him when I need my letters tapered because my "well" runs deep (as you can see). Just as he and others depend on my writing skills for turning letters from "**scratch**" into convincing requests or compelling demands, they will make you either despise, or oblige.

The only, major complaint that I have about "Mr. G." (with two miscommunications in nine years) is that he went-mute a few times when I thought that he should have spoken up. Very nonchalant in his personality and non-combative like me, I might not be able to depend on him to go to "battle" for me, and would end-up defending myself. Nonetheless, if it were up to most of the people in my circle, I would be married to "Mr. G.," and no longer waiting on *purpose.*

Once my sister suggested that he must be my "sugar-daddy." Most of the time, we were down at the same time, and came up at the same time. So I replied: "No, he's just a 'po-boy' with a big heart." So what's my dilemma now? You do not get married to be provided for, or even to avoid being lonely/horny. And since this book and a couple of others are about to "pop-off," the man I marry must be capable of sharing the **burden** of my ministry and handling the **weight** of my blessing. "Mr. G." often informs me that he is not going to learn how to be a preacher, if that's what I'm looking for. To set that record straight, I am not particularly waiting for a preacher; I am waiting purposely on that particular someone who is going in the direction of my passion.

Anyway, why must people view you so differently because you have never married? Despite the spelling, there is no sin in being single! Does it make people **feel** better to say they have been married and divorced, than to be single and waiting on God to **avoid** being divorced? Since marriage is so much more than just saying, "I do," or "I will," I refuse to settle with **learning** to love somebody because I got absorbed in a provisional fellowship, as opposed to waiting on a more permanent relationship. When "Mr. G" and I first reconnected, he admitted that he thought that I was going to be a "slam dunk" [sex partner]. He didn't realize that there were still so many "kinks" to work out. Those kinks ultimately were an indication that I was not the right link.

No "test-driving" here, sir. To take this "car" off the lot, you need to own keys that FIT the bill. Since I am not one of those women who say, "I'LL Carry the Note," my man will need to bring the title to the table as proof of ownership. And, because I am a considered a luxury "vehicle," he will need adequate insurance that would leave me with enough protection to cover me, in the event that he defaults on the loan. Remember, he is borrowing me from my Father who has taken exceptional care of me, to the point that I'm still not sure if I want to leave home.

"Mr. G." pointed out that I'm so different that he went out and bought a dictionary, and there was not a word in there that could describe me. That's because my difference, my faith, my tenacity, and my expectations are more unique than any, other woman that he has ever met. And because

I vow to "keep it locked until I get my rock," he also teased me that I must be a Republican because I say no to everything but money and food (☺). Then, he goes: "Why don't you print out me a list and let me know what you're **for**, rather than against."

Teaching moment: normally, if a man has my interest, my first question is: What church or denomination are you affiliated with? If he has not at least heard of COGIC or T. D. Jakes, it is a good suggestion that he may not be the one. My first impression of a man's credibility is not only determined by his emotional stability, but also his spiritual suitability. What a man is anointed to do is what I am attracted to pursue. "If you are not going to be landing in the same place, get them off of your launching pad," says Larry D. Reid. That's the difference in waiting for a Man **of** God, and settling for a man who vaguely **knows** God.

Furthermore, a man who has never heard of the Holy Ghost may make a good "baby-sitter" and give me a **feeling** of security. But I need someone who has the power to point me toward my destiny while being a good fit for my future. According to Acts 1:8, the Holy Ghost is the power source! A "curse-breaker" with power can call the hell out of "yo" children. "You heard me?" Taken from Trilogy-Part One, if you are married to someone who does not love and worship your God, by and large, your children are likely to speak the language of the world. Whenever "Mr. G." and I are eating out and he blesses the food, he closes the prayer with: "Pray for Karen, Lord." What was that?!? It always tickles me, but as far as my ministry, my destiny, and my "die-hard," holiness beliefs are concerned, we are not the match made in Heaven. We are great **FRIENDS** here on earth!

THROUGH THE EYES OF "MR. G."

From a man's perspective, if you would like the "inside-scoop" of some of my personal quirks, this section will express how "Mr. G." articulated them along the way. At this point, who would know better than him, right? First and foremost, since our friendship/fellowship has and will always be non-sexual, he stated: "This relationship is way out of line for me. My preferences and priorities have changed. I have never compromised my sex life, like this before. I must be having an out-of-body experience."

In his opinion, one must be a strong man to deal with me. Since "Mr. G." and I basically did everything together **except** have sex, he was only allowed to enter my "friend-zone" rather than my "inner courts." So, because he does not know me as a sex partner, he saw the relationship as complicated. At the same time, I engaged him because he was the perfect gentleman who never-ever, disrespected me. That's more than I can say for some of my personal encounters, **professing** holiness.

Rather than being, what some people would refer to as, "friends with benefits," "Mr. G." has tolerated my "friend-zone" because he can trust me. Under normal circumstances, he does not trust women, but I have proven to be so trustworthy that if I were to spend the night and needed to take something, he said that I would leave a note to let him know what I took. About 13 years older than me, he feels that trust is more powerful than love. Believe it or not, some men respond to sound over looks. In me, "Mr. G." hears the sound of honesty and purity, which is how the name, Karen, is actually characterized. Because we were always "there" in each others' times of need, we became friends in deed.

He says: "You stay in bed, but you don't want sex." In my defense, my laptop is my bedmate, and I do **not** want sex **unless** I am making love. That's the problem; there are too many people "making love" when they are not really **IN** love. That's not my story! The sex will come soon enough; you "gotta" be able to touch the heart before you can pat the "kitty." Never have sex to make love. When you are "paper-Bible saved" (as LRL would call it), sex is the act that comes as a result of right-relationship. Having only been in love twice in life, even a kiss by the wrong person will make me throw up in my own mouth.

Recently I was asked for an intimate kiss by a business associate. For starters, he hadn't even built up enough equity to even think about it. Perish the thought! If a person who barely knows me wants to kiss me in my mouth, where else will he want to stick his nasty tongue? With Covid-19 and other viruses spreading, I do NOT need to exchange juices right now. I know that I may be professionally-engaging, and even, physically-attractive for a 60 year-old, but is he stupid or what? "What the world; who 'da' hell!?"

I am not bothered that "Mr. G." calls me the weirdest person he's ever met because the Bible calls me a peculiar people. He feels that I don't like music because I complain of the noise whenever I get into his car. Being alone for so long, and with a passion for writing, I do appreciate a "noise-free-zone." I enjoy my own company, and I appreciate when I am able to clearly hear what I'm thinking. He also claims that I don't like the dark. Well, since I wake up with the chickens, way before the sun comes up, I do tend to wind-down, way before the sets.

Basically, what he is saying is that UNLESS I am away selling books (making money), don't bother to call me about anything else. He insists: "I don't care what day it is, or what time of the night – EVEN if you're in a wreck, you are not going to answer. Unless it's something that you want to do, you shut everybody out. If the sun is going down, 'I will call you in the morning'." "You are moody as hell. You really live in a perfect world because you think you can get what you want at the snap of a finger," claims "Mr. G." He adds, your "plate" is already fixed. Don't include any "dessert" because you only have a passion for what you want. Even if he invited me to go to France, he said my response would be: "Naw, I'm-gone stay here and go to **church**."

As far as being consistent in my walk of faith, "Mr. G." contends that I do NOT give up; I keep hope alive! He said that if Isis was coming to cut our heads off, I would respond: "Oh, they're not going to make it." Sometimes he will ask: "What's on the miracle-menu today?" After he saw me climb over the car seat to get out on the passenger-side of the car that my dad had given me, he told me to go NOW, and apply for car. With minimum income and multiple bankruptcies showing on my credit report, I obeyed "the Word of the Lord" and returned with almost, a new SUV. After that, "Mr. G." thought that I was a miracle-worker on any given day. He claims that I serve a higher power than anyone else. I call Him, Jehovah Jireh–my Provider.

After stopping by "Mr. G.'s" house one day, I asked: "How do I look today?" He goes: "Like a writer?" Me: "How do I usually look?" "Mr. G:" "All kinds of ways; it just depends on what day it is. Some days, you have on all kinds of colors, like you're having a 'I don't give-a-damn, day.' I feel like saying: pull that sh?$ off!" He goes on to say that even though I may wear rhinestone dresses from time to time, at least I have a pony-tail that's not fake. He calls me his pretty, sanctified, "childhood-hood rat" from the projects.

Whereas I decline certain activities because my testimony is that I am a sanctified girl, he has often asked me to **define** sanctified girls. "What do they do, besides eat," he asks. Me: "NOTHING." You see, by the time his folks came over into holiness with my folks, "Mr. G." had already joined the military. So that's why our core values differ in many ways. As we agree to disagree, he alleges that unless he and I are eating, I act as if he's contagious. My spiritual mother, Clarice Moore, always teases us when she calls and we are out. She goes: "I know 'y'all' are out eating." Always honest and forthright in his sarcasm and sense of humor, "Mr. G" goes: "Can you please pray that we do something else other than eat out?" She responds with emphasis: "That's what sanctified girls do; they meet up at restaurants, **and they go home**!"

On another occasion, "Mr. G." warned me that he was going to invite me to dinner, and when we end up at a hotel, I would ask, "Why are we here?" He said his reply is going to be: "We're going to 'eat'." But food was not on his menu. :-/ I "flat-lined" when he acknowledged that he did NOT want to meet any more sanctified girls! "You are the first and the last; next time, I'm getting me a "frucking" Asian woman!" Here is the point that he made rather bluntly: "This 'sh##' is driving me up the wall!" Once, when I rejected his "touchy-touchy" teases, he asked if I was scared of him. Me: "No, I'm just sanctified." He goes: "Well, let's shout about it." L☺L! The harder it is for men to get what men want, the more they want what they can't get!

The crux of the matter is: whoever comes into my life without Christ being the Head of theirs, they will always require more out of me than what I'm willing to give. At the end of the day, "Mr. G." appreciates the difference that I have brought to his discipline. He maintains that this is one of those experiences that he just can't explain. Let me explain it. Since the leading cause of divorce is marriage, and because my body is the temple of the Holy Ghost, I refuse to sleep with anyone who is not waking up as the head of my home. The gatekeeper needs to have voice-articulated authority and be able to speak the Word over my life, and when necessary, cast the devil out of my mind. Lusting for my flesh does not enter into the equation if he does not have the wisdom to be the watchman of my soul.

Did you know that your soul involves your order of reasoning, your ability to see the unseen, your ability to connect knowledge, and triggers and sensors that reflect your behavior? If you want a peace of mind, you cannot have a toxic person tied to your soul. Let me leave you with this before I get back to "Mr. G." You may be able to block a baby, but you can't block a soul-tie. Through sexual relations, you get to carry every one of those persons with you into the next relationship. As a result of you being a carrier, families become victims of all of your "knots" (soul-ties). Do yourself a favor; go online and watch Dr. Matthew Stevenson's Youtube message, entitled: *Knots*. You will what to know how to untie the "knots" and get your soul back.

To say the least, I can NOT allow my spirit and soul to get all wrapped up in another man's flesh! Moreover, I value my body/my temple too much to use it for "booty-calls." Romans 8:6 (ESV) forms a comprehensive meaning here: ***"For to set the mind on the flesh is death, but to set the mind on the Spirit is life and peace."*** Even as my friend's preferences happen not to be my policies, knowing who I am in God, obligates Him to save me His best. "When you start seeing your worth, you'll find it harder to stay around people who don't" (photo report). Just as I am aware of his desire for my flesh; I can appreciate the respect. All things being level, "girls want attention; women want respect!"

Even as I continue to evolve in my unique ideas for mate-selection, the point is, **godly** men fall in love with virtue, not vaginas! All things considered, "Mr. G." maintains that if I were somebody that he was just getting to know, he would have already been gone. Once, my fortune cookie said something about an adventure. He reacted: "An adventure? No, this relationship has been a 'roller coaster' that went up and never came down!"

Lately, he started referring to me as "Rachael," (my alter ego, I guess). As I now respond as "Rachael," he has warned me that if I didn't become serious about taking this relationship to the next level, I would end up meeting my "sister." After stopping by unexpectedly, I "believe" that it was the "sistah's" van that was parked in the driveway. While I needed to get something out of "Mr. G.'s" garage, he talked to me through the **crack** of the door, whereas he usually insists on me coming **inside** the door. Realistically, I believe that he may be finally moving on, but I will always call him my sexless friend.

Anybody who pursues sex **before** marriage is Satan's plan to keep you out of the presence of God. Be aware of the *false alarm*. While I am content to be single, celibate, & whole, I REFUSE to be unequally-yoked by yoking up with someone who does not share and want to maintain my same values and beliefs. The ability to use will-power over physical tendencies, sex is mind over matter anyway. If you don't think about it, it won't matter. Hence, I admonish every single person reading this book to decline using your freedom to satisfy sinful nature (read Gal. 5:13). Most men think with their head, rather than their heart.

Especially being called to a higher standard, being intimate for Christians goes much deeper than just having sex. After you have dishonored the God of your soul by defiling your temple with the desire of your flesh, do you ever wonder who and what you are taking home with you, once you have left the hotel or the unmarried bed? Whereas an exchange has been made, you have more or less, poured yourself into each other's bodies, along with all the other bodies that the both of you have slept with, and are now walking around with. I believe this one reason why this world is in the condition it's in.

Additionally, people's blessings are being held in "escrow" as their lives are in shambles because they are walking around and acting like all of the cussing, lying, cheating, fornicating, impoverished, disadvantaged, and "gambling-az" spirits that they have allowed to enter their courts (intercourse) through sexual relations. If you must allow other spirits to enter your temple before marriage, make sure that the exchange yields some spiritual benefits, and that their deposit makes a return that's worth the transfer.

By no means do I claim to be perfect, but here is how I personally operate: in order for there to be an emotional attachment or physical attraction, there MUST be a spiritual connection. However, when I was working for the airlines, there was this one, Black brother, who came through my line to board the flight I was working. He was so "hot" that I discreetly slipped him my business card. I was supposed to be making my final count on the aircraft, but if truth be told, I was trying to make a connection. Even as flirting is out of character for me, I don't ever remember being as physically-attracted to any other stranger as I was to this man. "O.M.G."

I believe that if I had been working in security, I would have **found** a reason to pat him down. A song that my Bishop likes to sing by Kirk

Franklin is: *Let Me Touch You* (and see if You are real). I KNOW that Jesus is real, so that song does not really work for me, but it sure would have worked for my passenger! Here was a man that I was reaching out to, to see if he thought that I was woman-enough to reach back. Not only was he professional, physically-attractive and well-dressed, there was something about his mere presence that demanded my **whole** attention.

In the history of my 11-year, airline career, my most intriguing passenger had a suave and aura that reminded me of former President Obama – a "whole" class act with no extras. I was hoping to hear from him, but I know me. If I discovered that he was not spiritually-compatible, that would have ended the conversation, and he would have been considered another *false alarm*. ***"Commit thy way unto the LORD; trust also in Him; and He shall bring it to pass"*** (Psa. 37:5 KJV). Despite what I might need, want or desire, marrying an unbeliever and being unequally-yoked is not an option for me.

The giants that the spies saw in the earth after the flood in Noah's day were not angels that God had promised to the Children of Israel. They were huge men (read Num. 13:32-33). The text is simply saying that when God's children marry the children of the ungodly, a confused and compromising way of life will evolve as a result. It "frucks" up the home, the community, the church, and most definitely the White House, and the world at large. #Definite"LRLer"

Also, in Deuteronomy 7:3-5, you will find that God's judgment towards the believer marrying an unbeliever has always been severe. A major reason why He has always expected us to marry in the faith is that **He seeks godly offspring** (read Mal. 2:15). When we obey and produce godly offspring, the devil knows that your seed will grow up and cause torture to the gates of hell. On the contrary, godliness is <u>interrupted</u> when ungodly men and women choose to create life outside of covenant (Reid, 2010). ***"Be ye not unequally yoked together with unbelievers"...*** (2 Cor. 6:14a KJV). Ultimately: ***"Can two walk together, except they be agreed?"*** (Amos 3:3 KJV).

Why Didn't I Get Married? Boaz or "No-az," I'm Waiting On Purpose. In making this commitment, I am being careful that I don't become a defeater of God's ***purpose.*** Though we are children of God, we can become adversaries even to that which God has called us to do. The Apostle Paul writes in 1 Corinthians 9:26-27 KJV (with emphasis added): ***"I therefore so run, not as uncertainly; so fight I, not as one that beateth the air: But I keep under my body, and bring it*** [force it] ***into subjection: lest that by any means, when I have preached to others, I myself should be a castaway."***

Simply stated, I do NOT want God to destroy my fruit because I did not obey His Word and/or operate in the function of my calling. Waiting on *purpose,* I refuse to marry based on my age, or that my biological close is ticking. Equally, I refuse to marry for the simple reason that marriage is a societal norm. I definitely refuse to marry for the purpose of having sex, or that the person I end up dating, **needs** sex. I will wait on *purpose* and marry based on "life insurance." Will my husband have the ability to cover my life emotionally, mentally, financially, physically, sexually, and **SPIRITUALLY**? Turn the page, and let's determine some criteria, "up-in-here."

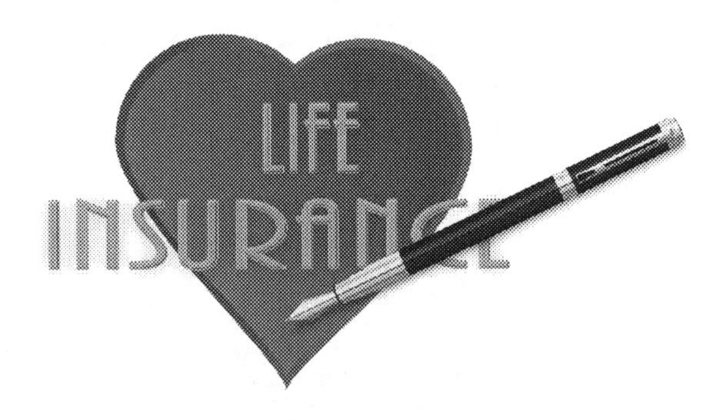

CHAPTER EIGHT

THE MINISTRY OF MARRIAGE

"So *Why Didn't I Get Married*? I am in love with me, some GOD!
On the other hand, I have the capacity to make time for the 'Right-az,'
only if he was sent by God to be my Boaz,
and not sent by the 'Devil's-az'
to be the 'Wrong-az' to make my 'Married-az' a 'Miserable-az'." #K.DR

Even as I am still asking (as a result of my last project), "Adam," "Where You At," I cannot settle for the suitable, and make a choice based on where I am. Why? What's suitable for my pursuit may be beneath God's standard for my *purpose*. Therefore, I must choose based on where I am going and not where I am. In the words of Tye Tribbett: *Don't let the now you, sabotage the next you.* You can't just marry potential; you must marry ambition! I beseech thee, my "sistah;" when you leave your father's protection, you need to know that you have a covering that is capable of being both **head**strong and storm-prepared. "Lightning" will hit your home, but storms don't come to stay; they only come to flush out the impurities. If the storm makes you break rather than bend, everybody will know how unstable your home is.

While you can never argue with a person's experiences, I captured some powerful nuggets from Tina Campbell. She stated, "If you marry somebody for potential, what you will end up with is their reality. You need to see some of that potential realized **before** you get married." In my final analysis, I have been forced to *wait on purpose* to avoid marrying potential. When you are desperate, both divine connections and demonic distractions look the same. That's how people end up in divorce court. They wind-up trying to carry out their divine purpose with people who have demonic assignments.

After breaking down the mechanisms for recognizing true intimacy, the clarity of criteria for who is the best "Adam" was complex but more apparent. Either way, I appreciate the status of being never-married, than having been married and now-divorced. Now that the wrong choices have brought me to the right places, never again do I intend to ask the kind of question that absorbs Part One of my Trilogy: *God, Why Didn't He Cover Me?* Looking back, the only bad experiences I have are the ones that I didn't learn from. Moving forward, I refuse to repeat the past that I have been released from.

The more you can be transparent about what you experienced, the less you have to worry about repeating it. Since my scars and experiences have taught me what not to tolerate, now I know what to anticipate. In other words, I may not know **who** he is, but I definitely know who he's **not**. Just as I am protected by *purpose*, a marriage outside of purpose will always bleed. Since safety is in the matrix of God's *purpose*, may I proceed with answering the other, famous question that I am so often confronted with? What are you looking for in a man?

Before the association and an affiliation becomes official, I have already spent many chapters discussing the spiritual elements. To safeguard me from ever becoming prey to deception again, I will conclude with the conclusion. Just as anyone else, I am naturally looking for chemistry. In this order, **C**hemistry must incorporate **C**HARACTER, **C**ompatibility, **C**ompetency, **C**ompanionability, **C**ompanionship, and **C**omprehensive **C**overage. How did all of these words end-up beginning with the c-letter? There is a **C**onnection here. In order to **C**reate, you must **C**onceive what is to be **C**onsidered. So in the **C**ontext of my **C**omprehension, these are my expectations of operating in spiritual harmony. If the standards are too high, no need to apply.

"Unattended meat attracts dogs," i.e. Satan does not care who we sleep with, as long as we wake up with "his-destructive-az." But when we incorporate standards with spirit, the Anointing (that destroys yokes) is increased when both people are functioning together in spiritual harmony. If I commit to giving **any** man delegated authority over my life, he must affirm me, by using the Word of God as the final authority in our home. If he creates <u>spiritual</u> intimacy in the relationship, I will not have to always depend on my pastor to intercede. I will know in my heart that I am **living** with a priest who can intercept the devil's plan to interfere. At the end of the day, my priest does not need to be a pastor, but he has to be anointed!

As discussed in an earlier chapter, I do not believe that opposites attract. If I believe in speaking in tongues but cussing is his second language, he will not attract me. If I believe in praising the New Year in, but he believes in partying the Old year out, we will not be able to agree on where we will spend our New Year's Eve. Tyler Perry's "Madea" said: "Your house is going to be schizophrenic!" ☺ If I believe in presenting my body as a living sacrifice, but he believes in defiling his temple with drugs and alcohol and premarital sex, I will be put in a predicament that will not lead me to a real priest. The point is: satan's initial strategy is to create a demonic relationship that will destroy the love that you have for God.

Now, can you see why I am so picky and waiting on *purpose*? A counterfeit blessing will contaminate my consecrated position. Before David showed up and Samuel anointed God a king, he had to deal with a bunch of counterfeits. How many men have you been dealing with, waiting on God's Anointed to show up? Aren't you tired of counterfeit blessings? The danger of staying in a counterfeit season too long distorts your discernment. The nation of Israel was a classic example. They dealt with so many counterfeit prophets and kings, that when the Messiah finally showed up, His own received Him not. Here are those c-letter words again: compromise desensitizes your ability to recognize the counterfeit. Compromise – Compatibility = Counterfeit.

Once, fascinated by a man whose sexuality was questionable, I dreamed about our wedding. Ironically, he was wearing the dress in the dream. I heard my granny say, "Baby girl, God's 'gonna' give you a **real** man." From that day forward, I was never fascinated by him again. The mister I'm waiting for is the one that my granny spoke into my dream! Years later, it turned out that this particular, public figure, publicly supports and defends homosexuality. In my best Ebonics, I "sho-ain't-gonna" compromise my womanhood for a man who is unsure of his manhood. To say the least, he would not be compatible to my sexuality. In my opinion, a woman who marries a homosexual or bisexual man, is either desperate, or she has no discernment. And likely, there is a part of her that needs to be healed. Likewise, as for the homosexual man who marries a real woman, Larry D. Reid adds: "What makes you go the fish market, when you know you want to go to the hotdog stand?" *-*

"But godliness with contentment (without compromise) ***is great gain"*** (1 Tim. 6:6 KJV with emphasis added)**.** After all of the years I waited, great gain is an indication that I am going to give some man double for **my** trouble! I plan to be able to say, I was "dead" in this area, but since you came into my life, there has been a resurrection. Marriage is a ministry assignment; the ministry of resurrection! What's not ministry about a resurrection? That's why you must always remember that the more you compromise your standards, eventually, it will suggest the level of your incompatibility. Ultimately, you will lose whatever you compromise to keep.

Get ready, this is going to be another fun chapter! I am reminded of a couple of movie dates I went on. When I had to ASK two different dates to buy me popcorn, I figured that they must have gotten caught-up in the movie and forgot to offer. Finally, when they came back without the soda to compliment the popcorn, I forgot about what my grandma had referred to in the dream as a real man. I was trying to figure out if there was at least, a **gentle**man in the house? Where in the "hood" did I find these cheap "jokers?" When a sorry "joker" is too inattentive to remember what constitutes a movie-date, it is a deviation from the accepted norm of dating. What is a movie without some popcorn **and** a soda, with your "silly behind?" "Where they do 'dat' at?"

Are you still wondering why I **DIDN'T** get married and am waiting on *purpose*? An acquaintance once made an accurate assessment in his observation. He stated, "With what you have gone through, the man who marries you has to be able to minister to your **spirit**, and he cannot be **SELFISH**. In order to satisfy you, he has to become you in his mind and make you feel wanted for who you are – not for what you have to offer." "What you had said!" I concur, but "if I am going fishing, I may as well go for the shark."

Overall, this powerfully-anointed, simply-attractive, competently-professional, financially-secure, wholly-sensitive, but amusingly-masculine, "**C**hrist-like" brother needs to love me **c**ompletely, passionately, and romantically. Also **c**apable of practicing open communication and mutual submission (Eph. 5:21), he must be skillful in giving me **non**-sexual affection. Worried about my sexual **c**ompetence? No worries.

I don't know what it is about these **c**-letter words; like the 3rd man in the Godhead, could it be the power of the 3rd (letter in the alphabet)? Either way, if you are truly **c**alled to be my priest, the emotional intimacy will "break every **C**hain" and **c**reate some unbridled, sexual passion that will give me the **c**apacity to make you say: "I hear the **C**hains falling." It may take the "jaws of life" to open me up, but once you go in, the "walls of Jericho" are definitely **c**oming down! Don't forget to bring the #ExtraVirginOil for the #ExtraVirginWoman. #wink:,-) Whatever works after my wait; I'm showing up, and I won't be late! ☺kay, I'm back. God orchestrated the "lockdown" so that no "locksmith" could decode the mystery without His permission. He has worked too hard and long to present me as a vessel of honor, to allow unclean spirits to pollute my temple.

Indeed, this is my idea of being **C**omprehensive without **C**ompromise. I pray that the "shark" sleeps peacefully and does not snore loud enough to wake up the whole shore. If you are aware that you have Sleep Apnea, just don't come without the **C**PAP machine; that's all I'm saying. Reader, never sign for anything that you didn't order, and always order what you have a taste for. The dessert will satisfy you, but the meat is what sustains you. I want my meat to be "good to the bone." "Yep," I may have some **C**harges against me, but pardoned for *purpose* and declared innocent by **divine** judicature, there is no need to "settle out of **C**ourt."

Coming out of High School and into my **early** adulthood, I could see myself settling because I still had time to re-do what needed to be revised. "Honey," I am in the "tweaking" stage at this age. Clearly, I am looking forward to retirement; I am not trying to come up with a new "project" after the two that follows this one. Learn the difference between a God-assignment and a satanic assassin. Do you want a relationship, or a "situation-ship." You don't get a receipt for taking the "wrong-az," and think you can return him in 30 days to request a "new-az." Perish the thought!

HARD QUESTIONS: To keep you from ending up "coo-coo" because you married "Boo-Boo," I created some questions to ask before saying, "I do." First, in order to do marriage ministry and not be miserably-married, you may not want to settle for someone who is just claiming to be a Christian. You and I may be of different, religious persuasions, but my initial question would be: Have you received the Holy Ghost since ye believed? No; have you literally SPAKE IN TONGUES, since ye believed? I don't need a man to say like the folks in Acts 19:2: "We have not so much as heard whether there be any Holy Ghost." **Wrong answer**!

Let's be clear, spiritual chemistry is definitely at the top of my priority list. So here is a Word challenge: Do you **know** the Word – of God, that is? Side-note: a man who is skilled enough to **apply** the Word that's hidden in his heart, is not afraid to repent. Nor is he intimidated by counsel. You do not have to be labeled as a preacher or prophet, but what do you have in your "Word account?" Next, what about communication skills? Do you know how to confront and talk things out? Or, when things don't go your way, you shut down, hold grudges and give your mate the silent treatment for days or weeks at a time? You don't live in a perfect world, so surely, you won't have the perfect marriage. Skillful communication, and even counseling, is very key to a successful marriage.

I know this next focus will fall outside the hallmark indicators of a polished author with four degrees. However, I am always willing to write "outside the box," to reach the one who's bounded by borders. As a leading inquiry to my next point, I need to know if you like to bathe. Since cleanliness is next to godliness, I object to a man that keeps musty balls and produce "doo-doo" drawers. @-) Forget that fluffy language, but that's a "whole" man who has not learned how to wipe his own ass; not "az," but ass (know the difference). By the time he got through replacing old drawers with new ones, he would learn not to throw his "**mess"** up in my face! "Ooops;" Lord, please prop me up on my leaning side because I was leaning toward saying the "s" w☺rd.

May I go ahead and "Karenize," contemporize, **and** modernize the rest of this for you? Since my name is Karen, I will do it without your permission. If I go to the hamper and the scent from the man-drawers smell "Zacklias" (exactly like ass), I'm calling a **complete** "FOUL." "What the world, who 'da' hell?" First, let me share a real intimate secret with you. To avoid being musty in the "secret place," antiperspirant deodorant works "down-there" in the creases and crevices, the same as it works under the arms. However, when it comes to the "breadbasket" (as LRL calls it), regular Wet Wipes are not going to "cut it." You "gone-need" some "WET-AZ-HARD-WIPES!" I'm sorry "bro," but a "raunchy-az" is a deal-breaker for my "O.C.D.-az!",-)

I cannot "breathe any more air" into that topic, but I need to stop and embellish the advice with some necessary commentary. The discerning of spirits is like the nose of the body. It gives you the ability to sniff out things that are not clean in the spirit. If I'm going to consent to getting married and giving up my space and my "whole" peace-of-mind, I don't need to bring ANY nasty-unclean spirits into my home.

At 60 years old, I am very true to what I commit. So if I am becoming a freak in bed, a cook in the kitchen, AND a maid around the house, we just need to get an understanding. Right now, my prayer-life and relationship with God allows me to **be** me, at any given time that I want to **do** me. Even if I get up at 4 or 5:00 in the a.m. and get in the face of God without washing my face, He still honors me with His presence. That's why we need to grow up and get off "milk," so that when church shuts down, we will know where to go when we don't know what to do – the purpose of building an altar before building a platform.

By the way, don't be so ambitious to go public that you forget to be prayerful. Personally, I am not aspiring to be anybody's coach, pastor, preacher or speaker. Honestly, I don't like people like that ☹. "God, just anoint me for the people-I'm called to." First, my focus is my relationship with God, and then, **writing** the vision for those who choose to read and run with it. I'm just not into the hype, the media, **or** the foolishness. "My bad;" before I got off-topic again, what I had intended to say was that once you give God your soul, He will never play games with your heart.

Consequently, the "11th Commandment" of a **large** number of married men is this: "Thou Shalt Not Get Caught." ***"Give honor to marriage, and remain faithful to one another in marriage. God will surely judge people who are immoral and those who commit adultery"*** (Heb. 13:4 NLT)**.** I am not determined to get married to any cheating man, just to avoid the stigma of being single. However, if he was sent by God to be my Boaz, and not sent by the "devil's-az" to be a "cheating-az, I will make time for the "right-az." "P☺W!"

Now back to the hard questions. Here is a question that I forgot to ask in the 1st edition (only a few weeks ago): What are your eating proclivities; do you value your health, or do you just eat out of control? I don't want a man that has the potential to become so huge that when he sits down, he's sitting next to everybody. ☺ If he dies prematurely, due to unhealthy, weight issues, I will need a Boaz to come after his "fat-dead-az." Don't mean a bit of harm; I just need to know what I'm hooking up with and working with, so that I will know what I'll have to live with, deal with and die with ('til death do us part). Let's have the "conver-dern-sati☺n." ("LRL-er"for-sure)

You are not on the Most Wanted List, are you? Do you have pedophile tendencies? Are you a registered sexual offender? Have you ever been physically-abusive? Are you on the "D.L.," or, are you just straight-up-"Sweet & Low?" With so many men on the "down-low" these days, "my-az" is not desperate enough for a "deceptive-az." Since the burden of clarity falls on the writer, and homosexuality is a trending topic, let's be clear here. While leaders are giving people the "green light" to walk in their truth, just make sure that you are prepared to live with the consequences. The only truth that will stand in the day of judgment is the Word of God.

I dare not judge the LBGT community, but just as I have addressed adulterous affairs, I would be remiss to expose my demons and not endorse God's deliverance. And since I am being forced to extend this chapter to an extra page (literally on the morning of submitting this 2nd edition), I may as well address what my cousin and I briefly discussed yesterday. While this discussion (brought on by a Facebook Live) was not by happenstance, thanks "Twin Ministry" for bringing the "hell" element into this equation. #WatchThose**C**-letter-Words #**C**reativeJuicesStillFlowing

Exactly "what in the wh☺le heaven and hell" is the whole point of debating whether there is a whole hell or not? "What 'da hell; who 'da hell!?!" Although I strongly support the Gospel Revolution of grace, I simply believe that the **C**hurch is dealing with the spirit of the anti-**C**hrist (anything that is against **C**hrist and/or goes against the knowledge of God). "But to whom much is given, much is required!" Grace does not change Luke 12:48.

I am living holy because it is written: ***"Be ye holy; for I am holy"*** (1 Pet. 1:16 KJV)**.** With six, other Old Testament Scriptures remaining that **commands** our holiness, I am not living holy, just to stay out of hell. My holiness is based on the simple fact that I absolutely love my **C**reator! Let me go ahead and hash tag this: #**C**hrist-**C**onsciousness-vs-Sin-**C**onsciousness #Good-Principles-vs-Bad-Practices. There is nothing that I **desire** to do that would give me a reason to look for an excuse to do anything differently from what I am doing.

Even in the **absence** of hell, fire and brimstone, what's so wrong with just doing right? Just the thought of being separated from the presence of my Father throughout eternity makes it a pleasure to present my body as a living sacrifice. That's the least I can do for the One who's done it all and given His only. Since we were bought with a price, we simply cannot do whatever the "hell" our flesh feels like doing. PLEASE read Galatians 5:16-17 & Jude 1:24). When we become new creatures in Christ, old things are passed away. Behold, all things are become new (2 Cor. 5:17).

If the grace of God allows us to be passive about our **c**hoices or whether we **c**ommit "sin" or not, then, why did John the Baptist preach repentance in Matthew 3:1-2? Why did Jesus preach repentance in Matthew 4:17? Why did He **c**ommand the 12 disciples to preach repentance in Luke 24:47, and the 70 to preach repentance in Luke 10:9? Need I go on? Jkay, I will! Why did Peter preach repentance in Acts 2:38, and why did Paul preach repentance in Acts 20:21? As a matter of fact, Paul made reference to the fate of wicked people more times in his epistles than he mentioned God's forgiveness, mercy, and Heaven **c**ombined. Since repentance is an indication of **C**hange and turning from your wicked ways, in some small measure, Karen D. Reid is just keeping with the **New** Testament tradition!

Also from my must-read, "Adam" book: "Some of us have no **c**onscience! We are ministry savvy, protocol primed but **c**haracter deficient! That's not a good mix! The healthiness of your **c**onscience is measured by the **c**onsistency of your enforcing the function of your **c**onscience, which is to provide constructive feedback that facilitates self-reflection! It's time to tighten up the loose standards!" advises Bishop Avery Kinney. Discipleship means **discipline**, might I add. Besides, why should God reward us for being disobedient? Do you reward your **c**hild for being disobedient? If so, that makes you a **dysfunctional** parent. The God I know is not dysfunctional!

I am sure that the "Hyper-grace Movement" would allude to this frame of mind as being superfluous, but I would rather do **more** than enough to make it in, than to get to the end and find out that I didn't do enough, to **get** in. "I **c**an't get no help in here!" Therefore, at the end of the day, I would still rather live like there **is** a hell and die and find out there is not a hell, than to live like there is **not** a hell and die and find out that there really **is** a hell. God will **not** send you to hell, but He loves you enough to give you **Choices**, as to allow you to send yourself to hell. My **c**onsistent **c**ommitment to God is this: I am going to do the best I **c**an with what I know. That's really all I **c**an do, and I believe that in the end, that's exactly what I will be held accountable for.

At any rate, "There is a new genre of **C**hristians on the rise! They humble themselves, they **c**onfess their sins, they renounce **c**ompromise – they reject worldliness and lay hold of the mighty hand of God! Them shall God cause to 'be strong and do exploits'!" (Dan. 11:32) insists Prophet Floyd Barber. Now that's the MOVEMENT that I'm a part of! As a whole, whatever our issues are, none of us (under **any** **c**ircumstances) should allow the lust of the flesh to **c**ontrol our spirit man. As much as we are in **c**ontrol of our **c**ars (when we are paying full attention), we are just as much in **c**ontrol of our actions. ***"Because He Himself suffered when He was tempted, He is able to help those who are being tempted"*** (Heb. 2:18 NIV)**.** Also read Romans 8:9.

ANYWAY, here is where I left out before I was tempted to get interrupted. SheNice Johnson stated: "Gays don't bark up trees that's not in the community." But if you are looking for a cover-up, "don't come for me" because you will get exposed by the light! And if you consider yourself, Brother "**BEEN**-Gay," I need to know if you have **completely** "**BEEN**-delivered." When I was a child, I spake as a child; I even enjoyed doing childish things, like eating "Sugar Babies." Now that I am a "whole" wo**man**, my "**men**-tality" calls for a "whole" **"sugar-free"** diet. wink,-)

Let me see if I can complete the following questions before you block and delete this whole chapter: How many "baby-mamas" do you have? Are you behind on any child support? Do you owe the IRS any back-pay? Do you own your own home? If not, why don't you, at this age? If so, is there a lien on it? Have you ever had a "prison ministry?" ☺ How many sex partners have you had? Have you ever had a STD or HIV? Side-note: some men come with baggage, others come with "whole packages!"

What's your credit score? Not only is a background check required; so is a credit check. ☺ Are you currently in bankruptcy? Since the woman has the grace to set the tone in the home, do you believe in being the sole provider, or do you expect me to work? Here is another one that I almost forgot: Do you have enough "wisdom" to save and invest, or do you spend and splurge without any discipline? Do you have life insurance, or will your family need to start a GoFundMe account, once you pass on? Beware of the guy who wears Rolexes and gators but has no life insurance. Suffice it to say that his priorities are all "jack'd-up!"

Here is are some mental health challenge questions: Exodus 34:7 claims that God visits the iniquity of the fathers upon the children, and upon the children's children – unto the third and fourth generations. Since it's the blood of the father that gives identity to the child, if you plan to have children and raise the next generation, what kind of bloodline curses and demons are you fighting? The "monstrous" truth is that you don't want children that are slow in school, sick in health, and crazy in life. With that in mind, let's talk about everything that runs in your family. Do you have **any** type of substance abuse history? From dealing with my own biological brothers, it is imperative that I know this.

About his bedroom performance, here is the big "game-changer." Do you need a "head-intercessor" to "work-it-up," "stroke-it-up," **and** "suck-it-up," or do you also need Viagra to wake-it-up? ☺ Are you "gonna" work with me, or not? If he needs all of the above to "pump-it-up," the work to "get-it-up" may take away my energy to "back-it-up." I don't mean "no" harm, but these answers should help determine whether a woman is willing to be tied to a man, "until death do us part." Did I not tell you that this book would be "blackish?"

That was the "big-screen" version of this crazy "reality show." Here is the "flat-screen" version that may cause you to "flat-line" right where you are. When you get through speaking in tongues, you may need to know how to **exercise** your tongue. If you don't know how to "bark in bed," the dog in him may not enjoy the "cat in you." Particularly when you do not have the skills of a "head-intercessor" (along-side the other, "wifey" duties), the rest of your life is a long time to tolerate a bunch of S.H.I.T. (**S**orrows, **H**eadaches, **I**gnorance & **T**roubles). I feel like somebody just pushed my "un-mute" button, but it was the church folks who taught me how to **spell shit and, live in sin**. And since writing is how I purge and get my release, help me to walk this on out, while I allow the Word to finish the work. ***"Being confident of this very thing, that He who has begun a good work in [me] will complete it"...*** (Phil. 1:6 with emphasis added).

Lastly, if you are calling yourself a pastor/preacher, you cannot sound like you're just getting started, or you have no anointing to continue. Around 60 years old, you should have been a novice, 30 years ago. Oh, that was not last; here is my "finally." If you are a controlling, manipulating, cheating, and lying, NARCISSITIC "C☹N-artist-az," I don't have time for your games either. Here is one of those lost interpretations that didn't make Scripture. Confusion is when a C☹N-fuses you into some foolishness! That will **never** happen again.

Manipulators hate boundaries! YOU have more of a chance at parting the Red Sea than you have at even taking me to dinner. I absolutely love free meals; I don't waste free, just like I don't waste $$. However, I can finally afford to take myself out to dinner. "The woman who knows what she brings to the table is not afraid to eat alone" (origin unknown). The point is: I refuse to allow anyone to take me back to a place that I had to fight my way out of. And because I have evolved, my life and ministry depend on all the right answers. You are probably thinking: "You may never get married." Well, don't ever fool yourself: "I'm good." Either way, my past has extracted out of me, that which would have prevented me, from receiving what really belongs to me. Kimesha "Kel" Leigh recently posted: "No matter how strong a queen has to be in the jungle, she always knows how to submit to a real king." Until then the "worst-az" taught me how to wait on the "best-az," to keep from becoming a "miserable-az."

All things considered, these are the issues that can affect my destiny, my ministry, and my peace! My "Auntee-mama" (Leora Hammond), often tells me that I can't marry Jesus because He is already taken. Just the same, I am content to wait on Jesus' "best-man." Although some women have the grace for a "deliverance ministry," my life has already been one disaster after another. Now, I am too exhausted to spend the rest of my life rebuking the hell out of a man. He can save that drama for his next "script," and save the baggage for his next "trip!" I "gotta" have a drama-free relationship with no life-altering side-effects! Seeing that I have a good case and justification for full redemption, I waited too long to settle for anything less than God's best.

This next section is going to bless you. David contends that the LORD is his shepherd, but for the purpose of this chapter, please absorb my personal proposal for the woman's Psalms, and allow me to qualify my breakdown of a man beyond compare:

THE WOMAN'S PSALMS

My **soul-mate** is **my** shepherd; he shall not
withhold any good thing from me.
He maketh me to lie down in green prosperity;
He leadeth me beside the still waters of the most beautiful beaches.
He restoreth my credit; he leadeth me in the paths
of divine favor, for his name's sake.
Yea, though I walk through the valley of the
shadows of my deplorable past,
I will never fear lack again, for thou art with me to provide for me.
Thy rod and thy staff will protect me from any
weapon that is formed against me.
Thou shall cover me and condemn every tongue that rises against me.
Thou preparest a table before me in the presence of my haters.
Thou anointest my head with motivating
words of wisdom and knowledge.

My cup runneth over with passionate lovemaking and relishing desire.
Surely peace and happiness shall follow me all the days of my life:
As long as my husband is my shepherd and re-presents the second Adam,
I will dwell in your house and never choose **any** shepherd over you,
until the day I return home to my Father which art in Heaven. #K.DR

That's how soul-mates do it, "Boo!" Just as my standard of excellence may sound like a fantasy, realistically, I must have a man who is more interested in his credit score than he is the basketball score. If my credit score is 750, what can a man bring to the table with a score of 350? That's like being marred to a comedian, and nothing is funny. Neither do I need a man who believes in playing the lottery but refuses to pay tithes. It is obvious why some men's prayers are not being answered – they cannot get their priorities straight. He has to love God more than me because if he chose me over God, he will choose another woman over me. And, if a man chooses a new suit over pampers for his baby, he will easily choose a gym membership over purchasing a life insurance policy. In the context of my standards: "Hey 'Adam,' 'where you at'?"

I would be one-sided to make it all about the woman's needs. I agree with the following list of 14 ways to give "Adam" what he needs, so that he does not mind being the MAN you need. (Taken from a Facebook post):

1. Never belittle your man.
2. Never talk down to him.
3. Never ignore him.
4. Never let him feel replaceable.
5. Never play down your need for him.
6. Never cause him to feel embarrassed.
7. Never look away or text while he's talking.
8. Never manipulate him.
9. Never boss him.
10. Never laugh at his mistakes or faults.
11. Never put any person before him.
12. Never be too busy for him.
13. Never be inconsiderate of his feelings.
14. Never tell his personal business.

Despite my autonomy and freedom in my singleness to patiently wait for however long it takes, Sommers-Flanagan and Sommers-Flanagan (2007) claim that family is a fundamental unit for human and cultural survival. A basic human truth is that: "We are born needing familial care to survive, and our species needs successful mating practices to avoid extinction" (p. 293). Even at the half-time phase of my life, the dictate of my biological time clock is inconsequential when measured against the backdrop of the Almighty. The unanticipated conditions have been cleared in my life, and the forecast is victory. I am next in line for take-off! The enemy cannot cancel anything that God has placed an assignment on. What has been scheduled for my life has been confirmed! My Confirmation # is Jeremiah 29:11 (KJV): ***"For I know the thoughts that I think toward you, saith the LORD, thoughts of peace, and not of evil, to give you an expected end."***

SO WHAT'S THE PLAN?

I was recently talking to my friend about some complications I was still having, since my last surgery. Bishop Louis Smith has always teased me whenever I was sick. He claimed that my "ever-ready," or sometimes "die-hard" batteries must have been low. This time, he told me that he was going to take me to the junkyard to see if he could get at least, $50.00 for me. He observed that I still look good on the outside, but I needed shocks and seats. After they placed me on the "rack," they would see: "transmission fluid leaking, a cracked motor, worn-out brakes, and that I was unable to go through inspection because I was smoking."

I asked him how much more could he get for me if I had a title? He said that he might be able to get $90.00. I gained a revelation from his amusing, sense of humor. Will adding the title, Mrs. to my name inflate my appraisal, or increase my value? I knew that my value had increased when I realized how whole I was without the other half. Still, how can I be whole, yet unfinished? "Something's missing!" Spiritually, I am whole, but physically, I am incomplete. Because I am spirit and flesh, spirit needs spirit, but flesh needs flesh. My claim is confirmed in Ecclesiastes 4:11 (KJV): ***"Again, if two lie together, then they have heat: but how can one be warm alone?"***

Since something's missing, *what's the plan*? There is no need in giving up on the God-given institution of marriage. Once we change what we are and become who God intended us to be, we will stop attracting all the "wrong-azzes." Although marriage is not a requirement, it is not good to be alone (Gen. 2:18a). "Woe to him that is alone when he falls" (Eccl. 4:10); you need someone to hear when you holler, "Help, I'm falling, and I can't get up."

Sometimes I feel my nakedness more vividly, than other times. For instance, when I pawned my jewelry for a prophet who continued to hound me for money, after we had only known each other for a week. Not long before that, I **LOANED** "Profit" Dale H. from Memphis, $1,000, and he later LIED that he thought it was a gift because he "preyed" and gave me a word. No, it was specifically for a project that he and a business partner was "supposed" to be developing. This guy was so scheming, he probably could have sold me an oceanfront without water. Beware! I call folks like him, U. P. C.'s (Undercover-Panhandling-Christians). Stop plugging into outlets that **always** have shortages, and get out of attachments that lead to subtractions!

While this "profit" has a reputation for being a prophet that preys on vulnerable, hardworking women, I can't undo what I did, but I **can** return the favor: ***"The wicked borroweth, and payeth not again"*** (Psa. 37:21 KJV)**.** I'm sick of the foolishness! Accordingly, Victoria Nicole Hooks penned the book: *"No Longer On Mute."* However, the shame is on me for not following the old, bureaucratic adage of "putting it in writing."

On a few other occasions when I emptied my account, I would say to myself: "Now if I had a husband, he would have protected me from that." Or, IF I was really being led by God, he could have come into agreement **with** me to make certain that the seed was planted in good faith. Whether I was hearing from God or not, the folks who accepted my money would have likely prevented their wives or daughters from doing what I did. He who has **no rule** is exposed to danger and is more susceptible to vulnerability.

So how can I make one + one = one? I must become whole enough to attach myself to another **whole** person. We should never connect with people with the hopes of them fixing our brokenness. As we saw in Chapter One, that's God's job and not man's. If your destiny is already solidified, the other person will only become a distraction if his destiny does not come into alignment with yours. If the other person depletes you, rather than completes you, that's a good indication that God didn't send him or her.

In my opinion, the right man is like the woman's insurance policy. Just as God gives animals a protective coating to protect them from their most dangerous climates, He gives the woman premium coverage to protect her from physical damage and emotional abuse. Such coverage also incorporates fraud protection and is a shield against manipulators. This high-risk policy guarantees the woman a second chance at staying in the right lane and yielding to the "**right**-of -way." So in order to function as one and support another person's destiny, at some point in time, I must step back into my covering and stop doing my own thing.

While vacationing alone, at my gorgeous 1400 square feet timeshare in Orlando, I realized how incomplete I was. By the seventh day of my trip, I was literally bored to tears. It was at that time that I admitted my need for companionship. Clearly, marriage is not my first calling, but since purpose is, I must confess that I have quite a bit to share with the man who becomes a part of my purpose. Now that my Boaz is on the horizons, and you are aware of my expectations, what will I offer him, once that special connection has been made?

Since my purpose is ministry and marriage is a ministry, I must be willing to minister to my man, so what's the plan, man? First of all, I will verbalize my love for him. A man must hear the words, "I love you." Secondly, I will praise him above every other man. Why was Abraham's body dead for Sarah and not for Hagar? Sarah did not know how to feed his masculine ego. By contrast, Delilah fed Samson's ego, but she baited him with her food. What you are moved by determines what you will move in-to. wink:,-)

Thus, the third thing that is on my agenda is to prepare special meals for him. "Nothing says loving like something from the oven" (7th Heaven). Even though I can cook what **I** like to eat and when I feel like cooking, I am not opposed to learning to cook whatever my man enjoys eating. Can you guess why? I realize that if he eats well **at** home, he won't be hungry once he **leaves** home. Since men enjoy surprises and love to receive gifts, that merges my fourth and fifth duties. Because men respond to touch, I must consistently touch him. Stroking his fingers, rubbing his head, patting his butt, and massaging his toes are just a few of the "appetizers" that will make me a "one-woman-wreaking crew." Lastly, I must be respectful and loyal. That means, not letting you in on the rest of my "full-course, carte du jour." I'm going to feel like I'm sitting at a poker table – I'm ALL IN.

After I get married, I anticipate writing a romantic novel, or a "reality show" that's quite the opposite of what I'm used to. Meanwhile, as a result of my influence on his life, my anointing should thrust my husband further into his destiny and push him closer to expanding his kingdom. He may be a king at the onset of our union, but if destiny has called him to be an apostle, he will be well-able to accept the challenge, by the time I have laid **my** hands on him. Being the favor on his life (as in Prov. 18:22), I will be key in increasing his prosperity. When a man is attached to his soul-mate, both his anointing and prosperity are intensified. David immediately won 10 battles, **after** he became involved with Abigail. "Hello somebody!" Promise has made an inseparable connection to *purpose*, when **your** plan is to insistently pursue **his** passion.

Subconsciously, we attract whom we think we deserve. One of the first lessons that I learned from Bishop Jakes (1994) was this: "If you are whole **before** you get married and not whole because you **got** married, only then do you become one flesh. A whole woman attracts a whole man; and when they come together, they create a whole marriage and produce whole children. If you are half-of-a-woman, you won't be attracted to a whole man. When he tries to love you, you won't like him. You'll like some dog that is mistreating you." "To be totally single is to be unique, separate, and whole," said the late, Dr. Myles Monroe. We are not ready for someone else, until we get to the point that we do not need someone else to make us whole.

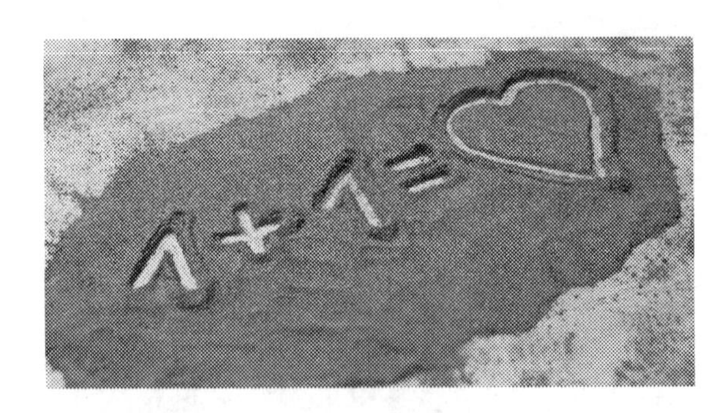

Marriage is simply, **two** single people who are successfully whole at being single. Your marriage will only be as successful as your singleness. That's why I have taken this time to get to know **me.** If your single life is rotten, you are not ready; a rotten egg only makes a rotten omelet. But if you are happy and whole before you are married, you will remain happy, regardless to what happens in, or after the marriage. Only Christ can make you happy; he that hath the Son hath life. When you possess the knowledge that produces the feeling, nobody can take that which is on the inside. When all hell breaks loose, as long as Christ is on the inside, you will always have a life. Popularity is people liking you; happiness is you, liking yourself. Now I understand why I demand so much privacy. When I am home alone, I enjoy the-me who is there **with** me.

If you are single and something's missing, look for **faithfulness** in the person who is totally whole and has found satisfaction within him or herself. That person has no need to look outside of him or herself for **fulfillment**. That's the whole reason I'm looking for faithfulness rather than fulfillment. Legal papers do not prevent a person from fornicating; they must be faithful and fulfilled **before** they march to the altar. Please understand: there is no keeping power in a mate. If one cannot live holy single, that is the one who won't live holy married. When a complete person in Christ possesses power over the flesh, that's the person who will be faithful to you because they are faithful to Christ first.

There are some hidden treasures left in me that are reserved for the right man with some power who will push me to fight for our future. But what if my soul-mate has married the wrong woman? Well, I can't punish myself because he didn't wait on God. What if he has passed and gone to heaven somewhere? I still have a right to be happy. So should I refuse to settle for anything less than what I feel I deserve? The following rationalization is the answer to my own questions: I have too much to offer, to die full; and, I have missed out on too much to live without what life has to offer.

So what's the plan? The suitable date that is not my soul-mate may not make the **best** man for God's **original** plan. However, being God's-next-best-man, it is possible for me to find enough love and security in him to commit to two things. I can be the desirable wife that will treat him right, and I can be the honorable woman that loves God with all her might. Vice-versa, he must be willing to make the same commitment.

In all actuality, I am definitely still single because of my expectations, especially since I draw such sharp analogies between the Christ and the man. ***… "Who is the figure of Him that was to come"*** (Rom. 5:14b KJV). Believing that God honors His Word to give me the desires of my heart and an *expected end*, why should I settle for anyone to love me less than Adam loved Eve, or the way Christ loves the Church? ***"He that spared not His own Son, but delivered Him up for us all, how shall He not with Him also freely give us all things?"*** (Rom. 8:32 KJV). *So what's the plan?* With strong faith, I am going to have a strong finish!

In the final analysis, "The enemy can't lock you out of your next level, but your access can be limited when you permit unauthorized access! God is changing the password so that hackers have to halt! Your assignment is password protected, and at every new level, God will reset the password! Get ready for a master-reset!" (Bishop Avery Kinney). Oh my! That was "powerful!" At this new level of my life, if a man cannot do MORE for me than what I have been able to do for myself; and, if he cannot help to carry out the good work that God has begun in me, I refuse to go in reverse to meet him wherever he is. Why? My pursuit of marriage will never be stronger than my passion for *purpose.*

CHAPTER NINE

DON'T ALLOW YOUR PURSUIT OF MATRIMONY TO BE STRONGER THAN YOUR PASSION FOR PURPOSE

"The judge may have legalized it, the preacher may have blessed it, and the church may have applauded it. But when your pursuit for matrimony is stronger than your passion for *purpose*, you can end up with a man who may not be your husband. Even though the church teaches that it is better to marry than burn, you cannot take the right methods and use them on the wrong person, and expect to get spiritual results." #K.DR

Pressing forward, I cannot forget to check his spiritual blood test, to make sure that he has tested positive for *purpose*. A man without a vision will not have much of **pro**vision. Connected to his purpose when taking on his name, I become who he is, and he becomes my *purpose*-partner. If he has no plans of moving out of "Lodebar," we will become Brother and Sister "STUCK-in-Lodebar-Together." A lady's man will pacify you temporarily, but a godly man will gratify you undyingly. Resolutely, if he cannot enrich who I already am, it is a lot less stressful to remain who I was before we met.

If your passion for matrimony is strong, allow your pursuit of *purpose* to be sound. Since I see myself in a greater light than just waiting on a man, my life is not determined, restricted, or limited by whether or not I end up with one. Because of the "Greater One in me," I am so happy with being me right now, that I do not want just another man. I want the Germans' inference of a husband (**hus** – house), (**band** – the band that wraps around the house). However, just as we noted in a previous chapter, I can be legally-married and still not have my own husband (priest, provider, and protector).

If I were to choose the wrong man, instead of dealing with my familiar spirits and tolerating my own demons, I will now have to endure an "alien" that will adjust and readjust my emotional temperature. Why? My pursuit for matrimony was stronger than my passion for *purpose*. By making the wrong choice, the enemy's strategy is to cause me to battle with the person that is closest to me, after I have become strong again.

Because the woman in John 4:16-18, kept repeating the same mistake in marriage, she was an adulterer – not a fornicator. When she did not marry **her** husband, she had papers on men who were designated to be husbands to somebody else. And as long as they were attached to the wrong woman, they could not perform their duty as the designated husband. As well, as long as she was sleeping with somebody else's head, she could not receive the whole covering or full protection because unequally-yoked equals inadequate impartation.

The judge may have legalized it, the preacher may have blessed it, and the church may have applauded it. But when your pursuit for matrimony is stronger than your passion for *purpose*, you may end up in adultery with a roommate who is not your soul-mate. Even though 1 Corinthians 7:9

teaches that it is better to marry than burn, you cannot take the right methods and use them on the wrong person and expect to get spiritual results. Sometimes, you must change the wrong marriage, in order to facilitate the right methods. Whose spouse are you really sleeping with tonight? When the natural and the spiritual are properly synchronized, a perfectly, marital union is harmonized.

I am not moved by every prophecy I hear, either. What some people consider prophecy is just straight out "witchcraft." Whenever another person is the object of your faith, you must consider the will of God and what that person's will is. Those are the two wills, along with your will that must be revealed, respected, and retained. Specifically, be careful of the "unemployed" prophet who sees you as his wife. Sometimes his self-serving will is to find a place to live. Prophets can seem ever so anointed, but some of them are only trying to find a sponsor at your expense.

Here is my point of reference. Once, I went on a blind date with a prophet, who could have physically, been a candidate for the Ambush Makeover Show at the time. Not possessing a phone, car, or a home, he had the audacity to "prophe**lie**" that I was his wife. Consequently, he was so unattractive that he would have been better off to wear a plastic bag over his head. At least with the plastic bag, he probably wouldn't have made it. J So was this prophecy or fantasy, or a "whole" lie? Was I desperate enough to compromise my *purpose* to pursue a so-called prophet? Rather, I made a vow to never, go on a blind date, ever a-gain.

Another prophet, ruthless in the Word, but literally toothless in the head, was so obsessed with finding a beautiful wife, that he could hardly see straight either. After an initial telephone "interview," I became his prophetic wife. While the world was asking, "Who wants to marry a millionaire," my dates were asking, "Who wants to marry a prophet?" My prophetic advice to this last prophet was: if you expect God to do the supernatural, you must take care of the natural first. Get your mouth fixed! While appearance is not everything, we need proficiency, production, as well as <u>presence</u>. You need to have more going on than the gifts because real women are expecting more than a word. They want to see your fruit! Likened to the Marines: we are "looking for the few **good** men."

READING THE FINE PRINT

I believe that love at first sight is possible, but I am extremely leery of men who propose to marry me after the first, few encounters. You may readily see a person's actions, but it takes a while longer to learn a person's spirit. As a matter of fact, the process of developing a relationship reminds me of building and/or purchasing a home. You simply cannot construct a new home overnight and expect to purchase it the next day.

In my opinion, the preliminary phase has to include time for processing; you cannot make progress, until you have gone through the process. During this time, you are going through a trial period – waiting and making sure that you have made the right choice. After your faith has been tested and tried and you have qualified for approval, you still need to wait a while longer. During this grace period, you will have to go through some changes, and everybody involved will have to engage in compromising. Then in the closing phase, you must complete a final walk-through and make sure that everything in the contract is signed, sealed, and delivered. Did you leave out anything? Is this what you really want? Is this really your final answer?

If snoring is a part of the agreement, you better, make sure that it's in writing. You cannot resell the "home," just because you can't sleep. Additionally, it is a little, too late to negotiate the contract by the time you become aware that he is a nasty-lazy man, who does not like to bathe. Neither will you be able to renege because you catch him drinking out of milk jugs and juice cartons. YOU MUST TAKE THE TIME TO READ THE FINE PRINT! This is the point that you will have to forget about all the other homes that you have looked at and romanticized about in your mind. Once you sign the contract, you are locked in, whether your "home" is brought up to code, or not. Once you fall for the "okie-doke," you are committed for at least, the next thirty years.

And if you are one of those people who does not believe in foreclosure/divorce, you are in it for life. This is the reason that it takes some of us longer than others to commit or come into a covenant agreement. In one of the most powerful books that I have ever read, Tommy Tenney said: "Sometimes the King **makes** you wait just to purify the outcome." Therefore, as noted by Mia Nelson-Tatum: "Excellence is not the goal; it's the standard."

After years of being single, I am comfortable with my routine. My spirit of excellence is displayed in ways that the opposite sex may not be willing to adapt to. I am downright dysfunctional if I don't make up my bed, first-thing in the mornings, even if I'm sick and getting right back in it. If the saying is true that clutter is the sign of a busy man, even my clutter has to be in order. In my opinion, O. C. D. is more often a sign of order and meticulousness.

Not only is money attracted to order, order helps you to sleep better. "It is the little foxes that spoil the vine" (Song of Sol. 2:15). A former roommate, who complained of having roaches before moving in with me taught me that life is as incomplete as the bed you left unmade. Had I not been insistent, that "unclean spirit" would have prevailed in my home. In fact, I have had two, very short-term, male roommates, and neither one of them gave me a positive spin of what it would be like to live with a scrupulous spouse.

I won't even gross you out with what I found left upstairs on the bathroom floor. L It mirrors one of those hard questions that I asked in Chapter Eight. Now I remember how and why that question was incorporated. One of my friends claimed that I had such a diverse selection of roommates that I should have called my services, "K.K.'s Extended Stay." Bridgette added that I should have applied for government cheese and a grant to buy more pillows and blankets. When my last roommate asked if I wanted to solicit for a second roommate from the local university, I thought, "I do not need any more 'unfamiliar' spirits in this house. I am having enough issues with the familiar spirits!"

After one minister asked permission to have a weekly, Bible Study in my home, Bridgette told me to tell him to put a steeple on his own house. Amused by her sidesplitting humor, she added, "Girl, you better stop letting these folks in your house. Next thing you know, you'll be walking around here bow-legged, needing an exorcism." She was extremely hilarious! I regret to add that she passed away, suddenly, on February 26, 2018. I truly miss her presence. ☹

Nonetheless, roommates were hard to live with, and at one point, hard to live without. Very responsible and calculating, most people who know me understand that I demand living in a drama-free zone. And I don't have energy for diffusing confusion, or allowing people to bring division into my discussions. You won't have to worry about me being combative, confrontational, or argumentative. I try to follow peace with all men; and if not, "dueces!" Even so, some people will mistake your endurance for hospitality.

The question remains: *Why Didn't I Get Married* and still, waiting on *purpose*? To say the least, I am not changing my standards; I am waiting on a man who can meet them. Sooner or later, he will come through like a thoroughbred. Once the possession is secured (as previously established), the focus will be on building a new home from ground-up, rather than remodeling an old, run-down structure. Maybe I am **too** engaged in *reading the fine print.*

All the same, I'm living alone and loving it! When a lady lives alone, she does not have to endure falling over in the toilet in the middle of the night because he left the seat up. She does not have to put up with someone using her decorative towels, or leaving their cap on the table, or allowing the microwave to remain nasty. Neither does she have to tolerate old dishwater being left in the sink, or crumbs left on the cabinet, or trinkets and what-knots being broken. Except having to share the same bathroom, these are all flashbacks from the one roommate who even washed clothes at 5:00 in the "doggone" morning! In **my** house, and in **my** kitchen, he even tried to dictate where to store **my** Dish Washing Detergent. "What the world!"

So let's be clear: if you don't think you can live with someone who has Obsessive-Compulsive Disorder (O.C.D.), I'm NOT the one. That's why I'm so passionate about editing, perfecting, preserving, and even recycling anything I can. You can see how I perfectly structure the end of my sentences, paragraphs and chapters and detect that I am precise and a woman of excellence. I told the Production Supervisor, "it's too much empty space at the end of that chapter; let's put an image there." As Bishop Porter say often: "I'm not new at this; I'm true to this."

"Mr. G." never understood why I rejected longer visits. As a mover and a shaker; I can't stand sitting around talking about **nothing** when I can be home writing about **something**. Even when I am sitting at the beauty salon or the doctors, I'm either going through my junk mail, de-cluttering my emails, or making collection calls for a friend. Time is too precious to waste; put some respect on it. Often, I must remind "Mr. G." that you cannot expect me to stop what I'm doing to accommodate what you want me to do, at the last minute. My whole week is planned the week before. In fact, my quirks and idiosyncrasies are so crazy that I have gotten up so early that I found myself eating lunch by 7 a.m. "Where they do 'dat at?" That's why it's so important to read the fine print and observe the way people operate.

So, with or without, "celibacy and single-mindedness bring the freedom to serve God in an unencumbered manner. A relationship with the Redeemer is divine" (origin unknown). ***"For your Maker is your husband – the LORD Almighty is His name" ...*** (Isa. 54:5a). Since my passion for *purpose* is stronger than my pursuit of marriage, let's turn the page and find out WHO is the WHY that has kept me from settling with the "Who-Know-What" or the "Wonder-Who's-Next."

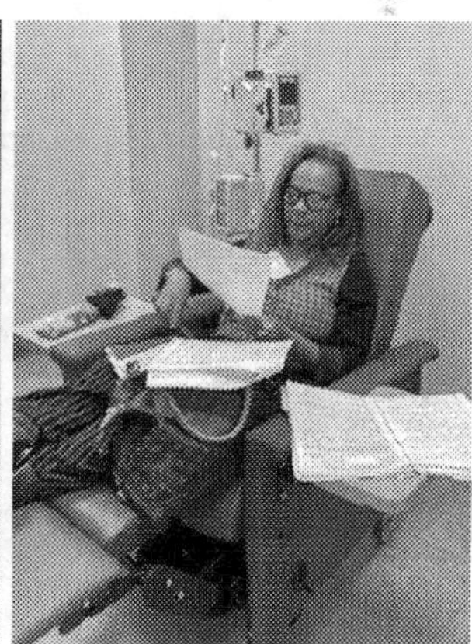

CHAPTER TEN

IN A RELATIONSHIP: THE BIG REVEAL

THE BIG QUESTION:

"Have I been singled out to become the Master's-piece because I have thus far, chosen the Master over the Mister? Or, is there really a Mister coming after the Master?" #K.DR

Now less than a week from going to the publisher the first time, I am not sure how these last, new chapters will end, but allow me to tell you how this one was birthed. Every morning, the 5:00 hour is my designated time to go to my secret place. Well, this routine was only divulged for the purposes and intents of this chapter. So on this one particular morning, I was experiencing the most intimate moment that I had felt ever, or in a very long time. At that moment, I wanted to express to the world that I was finally in an intimate relationship. The only thing that came to mind was to change my Facebook status from Single to, *In A Relationship.*

I received responses and comments from three types of people: those who were happy to see that my "single's ministry" was over; those who figured that my man is, and will always be, "Jesus Only" (despite my ridiculous claim); and, a few who were hoping that I was truly joking. Of those three types of people, the ones who knew that I was talking in codes, were correct indeed. My sister wrote: ... "With God forever! Congratulations!" (with a thumbs-up emoji). My spiritual mother wrote: "Thank God for **Jesus**!" The comments went on and on; a few of them were so sneeringly sarcastic that I decided to delete the whole post/thread.

Needless to say that in some strange way, I had mixed emotions. Since "I'm all-that" you see right there, why in the hell was it so shocking to believe that I could finally be *in a relationship*? In addition, there were friends like Donna Hardaway and Pastor Clinton Bryant, whose phone conversations made me laugh until it hurt. First, Donna's message went like this: "Now you know that I had to call you and mess with you. You know that **Jesus** is the only man that is going to be fooling with Karen D. Reid." When I returned the call the next day, she said: ... "Now when you get that cussing spirit on you again, just go back on Facebook and let the folks know that you are no longer in a relationship with Jesus. You are back to being Single. L☺L!

By the time we were able to stop laughing, logically I asked: "Donna, why do people think that I can't get a man?" She goes: "It's not that you **can't** get a man; it's that you are so independent that you aren't going to **tolerate** a man in your space." Okay, that made me feel a little-bit better. But then, this is how I was told that her mom responded to the news of me being *in a relationship*: "Who, **'OUR'** Karen Reid?" I was like: "Really, Mother Hardaway?" I went right back into my disenchanted zone. I said: "Tell 'Ora-D.' that I'm offended!" All in all, that conversation blessed me! I love the Hardaway family; we go back a long way.

So when Pastor Clinton Bryant first saw the post, he responded with one word: "Really?" The next day, he said that the Children of Israel had a better chance of raising Moses from the dead than I had of getting a husband. He told me to let it go. Then he goes: "God asked the folks in heaven, what's the biggest lie ever been told? The angel answered, 'there is no hell'." Pastor Bryant said that Moses' answer to the biggest lie ever been told was when Pharaoh lied that he would not let Your people go. Abraham's answer went like this: "I did not sleep with **that** woman." Here is where I "collapsed:" Pastor Bryant said that my Mama walked up and said: "I got one better than all of you; the biggest lie ever been told is when my daughter claimed on Facebook that she's in a relationship!" Sometimes, I can't take him! I had to get off the phone; it was ☺ver!

SINGLED-OUT

I will never forget the Sunday afternoon during a phone conversation when Bishop Craig Baymon suddenly deflected and said: "God is **in** love with you." My response, "For real?" I knew He loved me, but it was hard to imagine GOD being IN love with me. Not only have I come to grips with it; it has become my experience. For years, I have made a habit of spending quality time in morning prayer, particularly while it is still dark. But in recent months, my time of worship has gone to a deeper level. The only point of emphasis here is that God prefers private intimacy over our "PDA" (public display of affection).

Don't assume that because I am reserved and unemotional in public that I don't know how to "go-in." When you are "for real" in love with God, there is absolutely nothing like uninterrupted worship and waking up to one-on-one intimacy with no distractions. Because I am a worshipping cry-baby, I am reminded of the sinner woman whose sins were forgiven, simply because of her worship. Because this woman demonstrated her love the most, Jesus became the greatest Savior to the biggest sinner. ***"Wherefore I say unto thee, Her sins, which are many, are forgiven; for she loved much: but to whom little is forgiven, the same loveth little"*** (Lk. 7:47 KJV)**.** Even so, that's not even my main point.

Case in point: while her sins were **many**, she didn't even have to **ask** for forgiveness. Go ahead and ask me why. Real worship allows Jesus to honor you with His presence, hear your tears, feel your heart, become one with your emotions, read your mind, **and** answer your requests. Powerful! Without her having to say a word or make a request (vs. 48), He told this woman that her sins are forgiven. When you seek Him with your faith (vs. 50), you don't even have to ask for what you need. Matthew 6:33 KJV (with emphasis added) says it this way: ***... "And ALL these things shall be added unto you."***

Probably like the worshipper previously mentioned, my worship doesn't feel as real without my tears. In wishing that I was as close as she was to tangibly share how I feel, I heard Bishop Pearson say: "Tears flush the soul. The best therapy for pain or fear is to allow every tear to express its own story." Occasionally, I wake up with my heart and eyes full of tears, and even bitterness. These are the intense moments that I only feel like uttering my frustrations. But when the spirit is broken and contrite (repentant and regretful), this type of brokenness humbly expresses the need for God alone. So I ask Him to purify my thoughts so that what's on my mind does not affect my heart and interfere with my worship. I like how He validates me with His response, and then draws me right back into His presence.

I am sure that you are familiar with "Total & Permanent Disability," right? Well, in 2020, I filed for "Total & Permanent Deliverance." I may not be perfect, but my total deliverance has been granted from all distractions! In other words, the storm that left me torn is no longer my thorn. Absolutely nothing or nobody is worth coming between "the Lady, her LORD, and her LOVER." Oh, they still **try;** in fact, single/sanctified girls are expected to be "Freaky-Freddie-4-Free," where some guys like to come by and get their "nuts" off without leaving a "deposit slip." No free "NUTS" given here! We must **refuse** to be mishandled like a "bargain-basement-who'e" who refuses to say "NO!" Now is a good time to send out those disconnection "NO-tices."

They want us to take our masks off and "sing in their mikes" while they defile our spirits with their nasty deposits. I told one guy, "the only time I'm getting on my knees in this season is to ask God for grace and mercy." Like the saints used to say: "Come on out of here, you unclean spirit!" Who did Dr. Martin Luther King call the most disrespected woman in America? The Black woman! Woman of God, stop putting **your**self in a position to be disrespected! Don't be an "apple" that's an easy pick-up because it has fallen to the ground. Pick yourself up, and become a "peach out of reach!" Ask yourself this question: "You, what are you doing for me?" Then, ask the object of your affection, "What's in it for me?" Absolutely nothing compares with what God has for you. Keep it holy, and keep it moving! It has to be Him **OR** them–all or none!

When I gambled for a season, I would go for broke. So why can't I go hard like that for HIM? When your heart is broken into pieces, and those pieces belong to other gods that you are attached to, you can't truly worship God with a whole heart, and in spirit and in truth. You must consciously and consistently pursue the only-true and **living** God until you are coming from a place of deliberate wholeness and complete deliverance. The rewarder of them that diligently seek Him (Heb. 11:6), I want to delight myself in Him to the point that when I just think about what I want, He grants my desires on demand. Sometimes we get so caught up with what other folks can do for us, that we fail to realize how jealous God is.

"And do you suppose God doesn't care? The proverb has it that 'He's a fiercely jealous lover.' And what He gives in love is far better than anything else you'll find. It's common knowledge that 'God goes against the willful proud; God gives grace to the willing humble.' So let God work His will in you. Yell a loud no to the devil and watch

him scamper. Say a quiet yes to God and He'll be there in no time. Quit dabbling in sin. Purify your inner life. Quit playing the field. Hit bottom, and cry your eyes out. The fun and games are over. Get serious, really serious. Get down on your knees before the Master; it's the only way you'll get on your feet" (James 4:5-10 MSG Bible).

When I finally realized my worship potential, my position as a glory-carrier, and my title as a God-chaser became surreal that I started experiencing (in the year of the pandemic), miracles, signs and wonders. Not just as a one-time-Jesus-fix, or a week-end-church-thrill, being *in a relationship* is by no stretch of my imagination. It is just as real and addictive as a person being on crack. However, this glory didn't come without a price; it came with a consistent prayer life that forced me to build an altar in my home. Perhaps, the reason I'm still standing is that I learned to stay on my knees. When you do not have a prayer life outside of church, and you want to be what the old saints referred to as a "wonder," you become a ball of emotions, and not a ball of fire. That makes us all wonder "what-you-working-wit."

Back to me: I want my spiritual life to bring more glory to God than George Floyd's death brought attention to racism. Have you ever just wanted the glory on your life to go viral? That's where I am, and I believe it shall. I honestly want God to show up **for** me so that those around me can see Him **on** me. I am not sure if He has singled me out to be the Master's-piece because I have thus far, chosen the Master over the Mister. Or, if actually being single and more serious about my relationship has much to do with Him being **in** love with me. In any event, I feel that I am one of the ones whom He has *singled-out* to love Him back with a heart that is whole because it's no longer broken. Now you've gotten quiet on me. I can't begin to explain to you how being *in a relationship* has impacted my desire to enjoy this season of singleness.

Of course, if I had "played my cards right," I can think of a few, influential men that would have been willing to claim me as their bride. However, that's not what I agreed to, when I signed up to leave heaven and come here to fulfill God's purpose for my life. I agreed to conquer a personal earth-experience so that I could interrupt an ungodly, religious epidemic. Additionally, I would have only known how good a man can be to me, as opposed to learning through my afflictions, how great GOD could be to me.

To get to this place in Him, I value both my experiences **and** my afflictions and am thankful for every, single thing that it took for me to be able to complete this book. By investing in my healing rather than my feelings, the outcome of God's plan is that it prevailed over my pain. Always choose the right attitude, even in wrong situations. And, learn to breathe easily where you are, and be thankful for whom you have become as a result of where you **were**. As a matter of fact, it has been at least, three years, since I worked on this manuscript. But God would not finish downloading the message until it was time for the blessing (2021). "Timing is everything!"

Naturally, there are times when I feel like I got left out of the married loop, and times when I see friends and relatives enjoying their children and grandchildren, and it makes me "feel some kinda-way." Actually, it makes me miss my baby (the one I never had), and it makes me miss my Baby (my fur baby that died). I miss saying things like, "That's my baby," and "Good girl, Baby." But even in those moments, Jeremiah 29:11 kept me reminded in every season that God had a plan for my life. That was the season that He wanted my motherly-instincts to be revealed.

Just as things did not turn out the way I hoped they would, the silver lining is that I still look young because I didn't marry wr☺ng. No, the real silver lining is that God remained my Priest, Provider, and Protector. His Son, Jesus, is my Mediator and the access code to my inheritance.

And the Holy Spirit is my Helper, Comforter, and Keeper. Having made it this far without a "head of my home," what more can I ask for when the entire God-head lives in my heart? Even at "60," God still wants to make me His "Cinderella story."

While I am in the process of waking up to the dream of "going to the ball," I already know that the plan that God has is going to be larger than life itself. But I had to learn to manage His move before I could get my miracle. Absolutely nothing in this world is worth moving too soon and missing the timing of God. Whereas we waste too much time trying to do God's job, we must avoid being competitive and allow Him to be strategic. We won't have to work as hard in the next dimension as we did on the last level.

In the meantime, while God is keeping me all to Himself, I count it an honor to be all His. He may not always be my first and only, but He will always be my only-first. Looking for love in all the wrong places, I apologize to the men whom I held responsible for not being able to fill the space that was only intended for God. Looking for God in all the wrong people, I am sorry that I expected you to have the divine capacity to occupy a place that God had reserved only for Himself. While I was craving to feel my Father's inviting presence and to hear His engaging voice, I forgive myself for feeling irritated when I felt cheated on, lied to, disappointed by, and abandoned as a result of. Excuse me, I wasn't trying to find you; I was looking for God, my Only-Everything who would never-even think of forsaking me. "Thank You Father for wooing and welcoming me back to the altar where my spirit always belonged."

I have heard people say that God could never be a husband or a lover; I beg to differ. Philippians 4:19 supports the fact that He can supply ALL your need and be who/whatever you need Him to be. Besides, if you are a single person reading this book, you don't need sex now anyway; only married people need sex! And no, God does not take away the **desire** for sex just because you found yourself in divorce. But how about allowing Him to make love to you, as opposed to letting a man have sex with you. The Lover of your soul, God loves your soul enough not to break your heart. So permit Him to give you something to aspire to. The truth of the matter is: "the lack of true intimacy leads to the inability to connect in other areas" (Jim Carroll).

If you are single, say this out loud: "Father-God, if You decide to keep me to Yourself, I'm good. If You decide to release me to my soul-mate, You know how to take me from 'invisible to interesting to intriguing to irresistible'." Like Cinderella, you still have the "right" glass slipper in your pocket, proving that you are the one that your "Prince Charming" has been searching the Kingdom for. While that one man in a thousand is searching wide and low to locate you (Song of Solomon 3:3), you must keep that slipper reserved for the right Prince. That means, if he lives in Africa and he's walking, it might take a lot longer, but once he finds you, he will find a good thing. And guess what; that man will be blessed because of the favor of God that is on your life.

It may have been a long time coming, but no worries. Be happy that you are alone and not married wrong. During the recent, winter blast in my hometown, "Mr. G." recorded me in stilettos trying to walk on his iced-over drive-way. My friends couldn't understand why he was not helping me to my car. Well, one thing about it, he couldn't help and record at the same time. Here is the revelation that they failed to see: "you must wear shoes that fit where you are going!" I had already established that he was not the best fit for my future, so the ball that I am preparing for involves the "Prince" that can dance to my music. You may not be able to wait as long as I have, but stop being the "ambulance chaser." And allow this book to fuel your pause and provoke your purpose. If you trust God, He will make the right mate worth the long wait.

To the married ladies out there who have great husbands: honor them. To all of the ladies who lost your man: don't lose your mind over the one who left; protect your heart for the one who's coming. This is going to be a mouthful for those other ladies who are **playing** "wifey," hoping to become a whole wife. It takes too much energy to share your energy with someone who does not have enough energy to make a life-time commitment. Go ahead and **SWITCH** the narrative! In the words of Kenny Rogers, "You got to know when to hold them, know when to fold them, know when to walk away, and know when to run." That was a good place to talk back to me!

Lastly but certainly not least, if you are the head and priest of your home, allow your home to represent what SHOULD be going on in the Church. The world does not believe the God that they can't see. The Church believes God, whether we see Him or not. Thus, the Church needs to show the world that WHAT WE BELIEVE IS WHO HE IS. "So, Father-God, while You are saving each of us for our strategic moment in history (whether single, married, never-married, divorced or widowed), may we all know You in the power of Your might. And may we see You beyond our fantasies and imaginations, while hearing You above any and every distraction."

While You still have an audience Father-God, allow us to continue: "We will WAIT for You to perform marriages that You have ordained, orchestrate divorces of couples that You are not obligated to sustain, and overrule and overthrow any unnatural relationship that was never designed to remain. With a sign on our heart that says, 'Temporarily Closed for Spiritual Maintenance,' gut us out and renovate our temples, so that manifestation can be created as a result of purification and transformation.

Just as due order has been out of order, Father, make the Church in this season, a revolution that changes a people and a system, and not just a revolt that moves people in the midst of a Movement." ***"Blessed is the man that trusteth in the LORD, and whose hope is in the LORD"*** (Jer. 17:7 NKJV)**.** ***"And blessed is she that believed: for there shall be a performance of those things which were told her from the Lord"*** (Lk. 1:45 KJV)**.** God is not going to bless your mess, or send you His best, if you are less than the best than what His best deserves. Will you be the next "Cinderella," the next couple, or the next chapter that God uses to make His next move?

CHAPTER ELEVEN

SUCCESSFULLY SINGLE AT SOPHISTICATED "60"

Finally Dr. Karen D. Reid, Ph.D.

"Instead of shame and dishonor, you will enjoy a double share of honor. You will possess a double portion of prosperity in your land, and everlasting joy will be yours" (Isa. 61:7 NLT). #NothingMissingNothingBrokenNothingLacking

Never be tempted by what you see; always be disciplined by what you need. You never want to settle for immediate gratification above a long-term solution. Being older at being single and never married simply means that I have had more time to date and experience life, and to make a determination of what kind of person I could live with for the rest of my life. The more **mature** a couple is, there is a greater likelihood for satisfaction, and less likelihood for divorce.

In the meantime, I want to be like the diamond that Roger Moore mentioned in a Facebook post – "This diamond takes a lot of digging to find, and refuses to jump up for you. This type of woman can be identified by one thing. Just like a diamond, she remains rare. Some women may make the claim; but few are the REAL DEAL. The reason is, she down-tones her appearance to conceal herself, so that only a PRINCE of the MOST HIGH will find her. Needless to say, she sparkles when HE shows up because she KNOWS WHO sent him!"

Now embracing a process that I am invested in, it is through all of my childhood disappointments, teenage insecurities, and adult anxieties that I finally realize how strong I am. Why? It's because I remember how single I am. The question is not: Are you married, but have you ever been single? To be truly single means to be totally whole in one's self. I am not even asking for a man, at this point in my life. If you keep asking God for something that He is not ready for you to have, you may end up with what He gave Israel – a Saul for a king. Obviously, I see myself as the "Masters-piece" whose focus is to please the Master. So He gets ALL of me.

Single, Sanctified, and Satisfied–with benefits, I'm so single and whole that I come with a Bachelors degree, two Masters, **and** a Ph.D. Not only am I educated, I am a self-published author of now, six books, the producer of nine training manuals for church leaders, which has launched me as a Conference Exhibitor all across America. The CEO/President of my own, non-profit organization, my secular background includes two years of accounting, 10 years of church administration, and 11 years of customer service in the airline industry. As an accomplished, Black woman who represents well, I must say that based on the life events that I have juggled, I have made significant progress. Case in point: you must be overqualified where you are, in order to be promoted to where you are going. And, when you maximize every moment and optimize every opportunity, you don't have to settle for the "Sunday-School-dropout?"

Yet, even more than becoming both an "author-preneur" and an entrepreneur, and the designer of my own, custom-made T-shirt apparel, I simply pride myself on being a secret-closet worshipper. Preferring the testimony over any title, the essence of who I am is not determined by my education, my work experience, my accomplishments, or by my possessions. In connecting my identity to my profession, I must be able to remain a God-fearing woman, even when I can't do what I have learned to do. Whether I am *successfully single* or happily married, I want to display myself as a vessel of honor so that my **character** is what garners respect. "Hands-down," my main thrust is to be a trophy on display for the Him that lives in me. What an honor!

While there have been many odd, predictable chapters in my life, this is the chapter that signals an "**even** now" reminder of John 11:22 (KJV): ***"But I know, that even now, whatsoever thou wilt ask of God, God will give it thee."*** I am getting ready to "call it **even**." Things are getting ready to **even** out. I believe that the Anointing is about to double, doors are about to swing open, and I am getting ready to eat from the table that He has prepared for my enemies to see! I will go so far to say that in the year of 2021 (after 21 years of writing and waiting in obscurity), not only will this book become **my** best-seller; this is the season that will take me from imagination to manifestation.

At the time of the first, final edit, I went to the kitchen to take a break. I thought, "God, I am no longer asking or begging. I'm not even overly-concerned as to how this chapter will end." Then, I heard this: "God has already spoken; the only thing left for the devil to do is say, 'Amen'." While I am allowing God to do through me, what I cannot do outside of Him, I believe that "even" my "Boaz" may come **after** this! When you refuse to retreat, He will make your next, an "even-now" move. From miserably-mingled to *successfully-single*, the "devil's-az" has played all the cards he had left. Now it's my turn.

"Thou shalt also decree a thing, and it shall be established unto thee: and the light shall shine upon thy ways" (Job 22:8). Did you just notice the order of my priorities while I was placing my orders? For the right mate, I'm willing to wait! You can NOT lack specificity when you're placing large, personalized orders. I am believing that God is about to fill my order, just as much as I would trust the restaurant waiter to fill my order. You see, special orders take longer than regular orders. If you have ever filled out a Wendy's survey, one of the questions they ask is this: "Did you personalize your order?" The reason why my order has taken 21 years to fill is that I had the faith to personalize it, and then patiently wait for what most folks would dare to ask for. You best-believe that God has been working on it since the day I made the decree.

In the **mean**time, He has had to make sure that I could handle what I asked for. Again, I say, you can't get the MIRACLE until He knows that you can handle the MOVE. He will only make His big move on a house that is meticulously clean. **Even** while I was getting my house in order, He served me with grace and mercy. **Even** when I cried my eyes out, He bottled my tears. **Even** when I threatened to give up, He guarded my heart. **Even** as I dwell in the secret place, He keeps me covered under His shadow. In other words, **even** in my wait, He's had my back.

Because of my blind faith that has been unwavering for years, my sister, Sharon, the wife of a retired veteran, stated that she could **NEVER** live like me. She's got it like that! And as a result, she has been kind to her big sister. Not only did I **learn** to live this way; rather than the Hall of Fame, I chose to enter the Hall of "Survival-grade Faith." "Survival-grade faith builds conditioning through regular workouts in the gym of Scripture. Faith chooses to survive what it cannot explain" (The Cheerio Trail).

Yes, I am definitely a "church girl," but I am *successfully single* and a sanctified woman of God who does not use the song, "We fall down," as an excuse to keep falling. Sorry brothers, I am looking for substance, not sex. Meanwhile, "Intimacy with God through worship keeps you neutered until you are ready for intimacy with your spouse in marriage," says Prophet Floyd Barber. Woman of God, don't be a <u>foolish</u> virgin! If you have met someone that has potential, while you are waiting on God to work on him, make him wait on the "it" that he's trying to get.

Since Christian men often seek out the Proverbs 31 woman, we should make sure that they are Acts 11:24 (KJV) men. How does the Word describe this man, Barnabas? ***"For he was a good man, and full of the Holy Ghost and of faith" …*** Therefore, until our "finally" arrives and the heart is willing to say I will or I do, there are some relationships that we must be willing to pronounce the benediction over, in order to remain *successfully single.* Since God is the only One in life that I will ever again allow to use me at will, I will continue to wait until He is ready to share me with the man that He has created for me on *purpose.* God is so faithful that I am willing to wait in His presence, to be released to my *purpose.*

Conclusively, whether you are "the other woman" with a female issue that deserves a real man's attention, or a man that's willing to commit to covering the woman God gave you, it may just be that your female problem is all about your *purpose* in marriage, and your "male-issue" is about marrying the *purpose* of your ministry. Pray and agree to come to a place of rest and the assurance of salvation in a New Covenant relationship. In summary, we are coming to compliment you, so there is no need for us to compete with each other. W. O. G., do not despise the man's ministry; and, M. O. G., do not disregard the woman's *purpose.* Since ministry + *purpose* = a divine assignment, make sure that your mate is coded or built for your destiny.

Here is the final key that unlocks both the woman-code and the man-code: "Sistah-girl," if you act like a woman of God, you will attract a man of God! And "Bro-man," if you think like God, you will think like the man of God that the woman of God needs you to act like! How you get what you want is by giving each other what the other needs. Even as women are emotional, nurturing and maternal, they have physical needs, as well as natural needs. If you are holding back on the dollars, she's not going to be "willing" to give up the "drawers." Let me help you.

An insert from Trilogy-Part One bears repeating: When Eve was presented to Adam, he could already provide for her. She had absolutely nothing to worry about at the onset of the relationship. However, anxiety and frustration result when our needs are not instantly met. Eve knew nothing about living by faith until **after** the fall. Personally, since I have been living by faith all of my life as a Black, independent female, I do NOT expect to leave a lavish wedding ceremony and go home to another *luxury* apartment. That's not hot, and that's not God!

After ALL I have been through to get to my "go-T☺," my Father, my daddy, and my "sister-nem" need to know that where my husband is taking me the day I say "I do," is not the same places that I have already traveled through! With humble gratitude, I am already living in an apartment with granite counter tops, stainless steel sink and appliances, and a balcony view of a beautiful swimming pool. While I have managed to live like this on a "shoe-string" budget (I do not despise small beginnings or living by faith), but I deserve much more than this. So in my new world, a downgrade is a deal-breaker. At this point, Y☺U are required to be the "come-up!"

While I was praying and waiting on my "Boo," he should have been planning and working toward my "hither-TO." ... If my "Boo" is unable to enlarge my borders, then, my "Boo" is not my Boaz. In modeling the importance of being a real man, you must think like Adam in order for me to live like Eve (Reid, 2010). *Successfully single* and waiting on *purpose*, I'm Karen D. Reid (K.DR), and my Lover (the LORD) approves this message.

NEWSBREAK:
THE PANDEMIC PRAISE REPORT

WAIT A MINUTE! Did I attempt to close this book in faith-mode and STILL believing God to fill my special orders? "My bad." I would not have been able to call myself, *Successfully Single At Sophisticated "60"* (as of January 17, 2021), and publish this book in good conscious without some kind of "successfully-single" manifestation. No, I am still not so rich in material possessions, but what I have gained is **wealth in my perception and satisfaction in my contentment**. So accustomed to over-investing in things that make me **look or feel** successful, it has taken me all of these years and chapters to realize that I do not have to be rich to be wealthy. Doing better with less, New York Times, Best-Selling author, Greg McKeown, calls it the *Disciplined Pursuit of Less*; it is the way of the *Essentialist.*

Literally, my ongoing, financial situation had kept me in the "wilderness" for the past 40 years. But during the year of the pandemic, I have produced less, while doing better in making the highest-natural progression. Having totally mastered sacrificial giving (without even working), I can imagine how Joseph felt when he called his firstborn Manasseh, and the second, Ephraim (Gen. 41:51-52). God has made me forget all my toil and has caused me to be fruitful in the land of my affliction. Psalm 37:19 (NLT) became my testimony in 2020: ***"They will not be disgraced in hard times; even in famine they will have more than enough."***

In gaining and claiming control of my own choices to make the highest-possible contributions to what is absolutely essential, there were three obvious lessons that I needed to learn to get from way-back-there, to all-the-way-here:

(1) After adopting a financial wellness plan, I had to learn how to tithe and GIVE correctly. Even as my personal ministry suffers from a lack of support, I still believe in sowing <u>outwardly</u>. However, I recently had the epiphany that if I don't start investing in my own vision, I am only helping others to build their ministry empires. I will always lack funds for projects, revisions, expansions, coaching, marketing, travel, exhibit fees, etc. These are funds that have been coming out of my personal "coins," but that's CHANGING!

Often feeling like the biggest giver, but the biggest loser, I'm not becoming self-centered; I'm just becoming more self-conscious. Even as a college student, I would give away my grant money to anyone I saw with a need. I went as far as purchasing cars for people; not to mention the tens of thousands of dollars that I have given to both ministries and individuals. And even now, not only will I give to a stranger that's playing a harp in the heat; I have found myself looking for stray dogs to feed on the streets.

I had to learn that just because I have money is no indication that God gave it to me to give it away. Besides, if you make people aware of what you have, they will expect favors **from** you that they wouldn't even be willing to return **to** you. Question: Why do some people get blessed (more often than people who deserve to get blessed), don't get blessed? Answer: Often, God will refrain from blessing your income until **YOU** find a way to hone in on your gifts and **maximize** what **you** have coming in.

(2) Having had a lottery mentality throughout my adult life, I also learned to stop fantasizing and start recognizing. I could not keep chasing my fantasies, waiting on them to turn into realities. Rather, I had to turn my focus to relationship and pure worship. When I started to worship God because I love Him, and not because of what I needed **from** Him, Psalm 23:1 became my attitude: "The LORD is my Shepherd, I shall not want." Why is **just** God, not enough? Since absolutely nothing is more powerful, whatever happened to **just** speaking and obeying the Word? Now, I focus on **just** three things. I seek first the kingdom of God, and

His righteousness... (Mt. 6:33). I delight myself also in the LORD ... (Psa. 37:4); and, I set my affections on things above ... (Col. 3:2).

Do you know what these behavioral, attitude and Word changes literally do for me? They give me access to what's already mine. I totally believe in the prophetic, and it absolutely amazes me when I get an indisputable prophecy. Yet, according to John 15:7, when I abide in Him and His Words abide in me, I really don't need a prophecy or a miracle. I can ask what I will, and it shall be done unto me! I don't have to work for it, seek after it, or even try to pay for it. Why not? The promises are activated by the Word of God.

In Romans 8:32, He promised to **freely** give us all things, so why should I allow antics and tactics to manipulate me to receive the blessings that already belong to me (Eph. 1:3)? Also read Colossians 3:23. Some of these church scammers are so convincing, and will say whatever they think you need to hear, while knowing that their motive is to talk you out of your money. Some are already millionaires; why do they continue to beg and solicit as if it's only about the seed? Just be honest; it's also about fattening your pockets!

I have seen prophets die prematurely; I believe it may have been as a result of "stealing the sacred." You cannot continue to manipulate God's people out of their hard-earned money and be seen in Vegas gambling it away. "What the hell!?!" Of course, when we have a marketplace anointing incorporated with right motives, we **should** learn to pivot our prophetic brands with prophetic marketing strategies. Yet, real **ministry** should be a passion, and never a grind and a hustle, or **seductive** marketing where the object of your focus ushers in a spirit that turns cheerful giving into conniving takings. "GIVE US A BREAK!" We are in a pandemic! Indeed, giving is always a huge part of worship, but people give cheerfully when not under pressure.

Check this out: ***"Then they asked Him, 'What must we do to do the works GOD requires?' Jesus answered, 'The work of GOD is this: to believe in the One HE has sent'."*** (John 6:28-29 NIV with emphasis added). God does not want us making IDOLS out of people and their MINISTRY gifts, whereas we start relying on them, rather than depending on Him. In harmony with Damion Orlando Archat: "Good marketing has the Church following rebranded witchcraft. And it's easier to follow rebranded witchcraft than it is to follow the simple principles of God."

Just as the Cash App has become the new offering plate, and everybody is looking for new ways to survive the pandemic, why don't we start a different kind of Facebook Challenge? In order to guard your spirit, heart, soul **and** pocket, allow **your** face to get in HIS Book! Keep in mind that when you move out of God's face, you move into the wrong place (places of lust, pride, greed and competition).

(3) Lastly, I had to learn to stop casting my pearls before swine. Enough is enough! I never demand anything from anybody; neither do I give with the expectation of reciprocation. But the people I despise are those who feel entitled to your blessings, but try to conceal their blessings to avoid sharing with the people who have been there for them. For instance: After supporting this one couple and helping to get their car out of repo, they later stopped by my place to show off their new vehicle with no mention of keeping the word that "he" made so passionately. Here is the kicker. They stopped by again and couldn't wait to get back to their car to gobble down food that they were too selfish to share. While eating like they were coming off of a long consecration, they never knew that I was watching them from my upstairs window. ☹

And then there are those other people who never ask what can I do for you, **unless** it benefits them. Being that I am so independent and accustomed to making things happen for myself, I really **don't** care whether people oblige me or not. But it's just the nature of the Father that we have the need to feel appreciated. Sometimes, I **test** the folks who always expect something for nothing, just to see if they think as much of me as I think of them. And they don't even realize that a simple request was only a test. The point of this whole rant is this: dumb swine think that you are throwing stones at it because they are too dumb to recognize the value of your pearls.

Not that I **need** the "swine" to reciprocate, but in the event that they **need** my "stones" again, they simply **need** to learn the **value** of my "pearls." Yet, there is the five, faithful few, who, with no special occasion needed, have <u>consistently</u> come through and reminded me that my gift/ministry is not invisible. You know who you are; and please know that I appreciate what you do. I guess the difference in being a paid consultant and a "non-profit" organization is discerning your own worth to the people who are determined to take it for granted. At the end of the day, concern yourself with the people who care, and "attend to the business that pays the bills" (Tiphani Montgomery).

Let me get out of my feelings and get back into the Spirit. I started this section talking about what it took for me to become an Essentialist. Before God could trust me to manage the miracle of millions, I had to learn that every need is NOT my assignment. And I had to learn that my personal blessings are NOT always "group blessings." Otherwise, the same way that I remained in poverty with the least, I would end-up in poverty with the most. I also had to learn the difference between need and greed. If your field is fruitful enough for people to prosper off your seed, make sure their ground is fertile enough to yield a harvest.

In 2020, the year of double vision, both of my eyes came opened! I do not label myself as a prophet or a seer, but when I disallow my **emotions** to cloud my judgment, discernment kicks in and allow me to see what I need to see and hear what I need to hear. Sometimes, God will even speak to you through the television. Near the conclusion of completing this book, God allowed me to hear (loud and clear), the very end of a commercial that I was not even paying attention to. The person said: "Your sacrifices have not been forgotten." That blessed me! I took it personal!

The actual day before I submitted this project the first time, the amazing Prophet Prempeh, signaled me out on his Zoom platform. He saw a jar filled to the top with water, but it had no leakage. He said that my destiny was sealed, but there had been delays and circumstances that prevented it from being released or leaking out. Now that I have discussed what I feel were some of the reasons **for** my delays, allow me to conclude with the *Pandemic Praise Report.* Rather than spreading my efforts, energies, and resources too thin as a consequence of **emotional giving**, the testimony is: I now give greater precision to both who and what really matters. As a result of **emotional management**, the critical clarity of focus, and the impact of my blessings, productivity, and well-being, are **PROFOUND**.

Because Azusa was both my "go-to" and Exodus when I first started my deliverance process, I recently expressed a desire to Bishop Carlton Pearson to sow into his Facebook, Azusa Revisit platform. However, I told him that since I had recently planted thousands of dollars into some other platforms, I needed time to recover. Since Azusa had been what I refer to as my "heaven on earth," I wanted my seed to make an impact. This is how he responded: "God knows and sees your precious heart. Don't feel pressured. We do what we can, and God does what we can't"

His honorable response makes it an HONOR to give. Later, I explained some concerns to my favorite vlogger, whom I had largely supported as a result of him sounding the alarm on some of this "frucking niggament." He replied: "I can NEVER tell anyone to stop sowing...BUT I will say to you that you should hold to your savings and all monies. The only time you go in it is when you feel led to give; I mean REALLY have a leading. Take time and build" ... Wow!

By the way, why do I support Larry Reid Live, one may ask? Not only is he entertaining, educational and empowering. He is doing with his platform what I tried to do with my Trilogy, *From Mistress To Ministry*, almost 20 years ago. While God has finally groomed somebody to give voice to many of our stories, some leaders refused to associate themselves with my "testimony" because coming against premeditated sin would have been going against their "wrong-az" friend! Just as I said in my Trilogy, Part One, we cannot save the world until God purifies the Church!

"Why should you be stricken and punished again [since no change results from it]? You [only] continue to rebel. The whole head is sick And the whole heart is faint and sick" (Isa. 1:5 AMP)**.** ***"I hate, I despise your religious festivals; your assemblies are a stench to me.... Though you bring choice fellowship offerings, I will have no regard for them. Away with the noise of your songs! I will not listen to the music of your harps. But let justice roll on like a river" ...*** (Amos 5:21-24 NIV)**.** Does this even sound familiar? Has Covid-19 taught us anything beyond power, money and sex (P.M.S.)? Generally speaking, we're not ready for revival. Why not? ***"For the time is come that judgment MUST begin at the house of God"*** (1 Pet. 4:17 KJV with special emphasis)**.** And that's why I support "Jeremy" Reid; it's pers☺nal!

Oh, before I was interrupted again, here is where I left off. In any case, money is a defense because it builds a fortress around your heart. There has been the tendency to say that money changes people. No, for those who can handle it, it helps you to see change. Otherwise, it exposes and magnifies greed in the person who already has the proclivity to become greedy. Thus, God cannot pour a gallon-size blessing into a pint-size mentality. What you do with little determines how much He will trust you with much. I rarely believe the hype when people claim what they will do for me if they hit it big. "Talk is cheap;" it's easy to say what you will do with money in your mind that you do not have in your hands. Likely, people will do just what they are doing now. If you give big with little, the more you will give when you come into much.

In any event, here is what the 2020 Covid-19 Pandemic has revealed to me: I don't have to have what I thought that I couldn't live without, and I really don't need what I thought I wanted. To be successful, you first must have the capacity to do without. Then God gives you the grace to know when to give and how to maintain. ***"Then Isaac sowed in that land, and received in the same year*** [of the famine] ***an hundredfold: and the LORD blessed him"*** (Gen. 26:12 KJV with emphasis added)**.** Rather than pursuing things that would make it **look** like I had won over my enemies, the *Pandemic Praise Report* is that I have been successful enough to **"P.I.F."** the debts that made success not so successful.

FROM FIGHT TO FAVOR

I have finally gone from never-enough, to almost-just-enough, to now, MORE-THAN-ENOUGH. Recently, I reconnected with an acquaintance who recalled taking me to the bank to make a $5 deposit. I am positive that it was to keep a check from bouncing. I remember the look on his face, when he asked: "Are you serious?" He was not only embarrassed, he admitted to being horrified to hand the teller a $5 deposit. Worried about his reputation, he said his prayer was: "God, if this woman ever needed you before, she needs you now."

Sarcastically, Pastor Quinn recently added that he needed counseling after that and had to go into solitude. #hilarious Then, I mentioned to him that a few days before when my aunt called, she couldn't believe that I was in the process of making a $30 deposit. He goes: "The Lord is blessing; at least you went up." Since my heartstrings were attached to my Cash App account, I had emptied it to make my 2nd-largest donation to-date. So, to avoid easy access to spontaneous giving that could become a flesh-move, I limited this account to paying monthly expenses.

Looking back at when I could barely afford to buy toilet tissue, my comedic-pastor friend (Bryant) once said: "Don't tell folks that you're a Christian. If God can't take no better care of you than that, tell them that you are Hindu, Muslim, Harry Krishner, Sung Young Moon, Buddhist, or a survivor of Jim Jones. You hurt the cause of Christ!" I laughed uncontrollably! Whenever I'm sick, he often teases me that I refuse to die. You have to know the inside joke to appreciate that statement. He claims that if I had been a part of the Jonestown Massacre, knowing my good luck, by the time I went to the bathroom and came out, all of the Kool-Aid would have been gone. And I would've be like: 'What happened? Why-everybody-all laid ☺ut'?"

Recently, when I told him that I had plenty of tissue, he goes: "And the Church of Christ folks don't believe that God is still working miracles. That's right up there with the Red Sea crossing." Connected to my work more than the potential wealth, I humbly told him that I was working on my 15th book (including training manuals). He goes: ... "Fifteen books with a **net gain** of $15!" Before 2019, he would have **not** been too far from the truth, technically. Yet, my ministry has never been about the money, but about the moment. *From fight to favor*, this is only a reflection of how far I have come, and a mere preview of a coming attraction.

Believe it or not, I still have three bankruptcies (three separate filings for the same bankruptcy–if that makes sense), attached to my credit file. Yet, at the time of this writing, I have managed to raise my credit score to almost 750. I call it, "Walking in the F.O.G." (favor of God). When Costco couldn't take a certain credit card the other day, I was able to flip to a debit card that has enough money to spend what I want, when I want, and never stop to check the balance. *From fight to favor*, that's my idea of being *successfully single at sophisticated "60."* Just as this assignment is so much bigger than me, the point here is that there is absolutely nothing that you can worry about that God is not bigger than.

FROM OVERDRAFT TO OVERFLOW

Here is where I assessed my immediate state of affairs. No matter how many trunk-loads I give away, or how many suits I sell with tags still on them, I have always had clothes "out-the-wazoo." But here come the clinchers. When I always struggled to pay a single, phone bill, I now have three, cell phones. Whereas I was forced to take advantage of high-risk credit card invitations with high-interest rates, I now have emergency credit cards with zero balances. When extensions were my monthly norm, I no longer carry a balance on my Light, Gas & Water bill.

Wait! God has miraculously expanded my health insurance, to the point where I have no more $40 specialist co-pays. While checking in at my last two doctors' visits, I was like: HOW/when did that happen? That was one of those "sweatless" victories that I stopped trying to figure out. I told myself; "just use it before you lose it!" Since I no longer have to "borrow from Peter to pay Paul," I'm **never** late on rent. Pawn shops and title loans are a **curse** of the past. Rather than always driving near E (exhausted), I **never** purchase gas without filling up. Yesterday, when I went to fill up, I gasped when I noticed that the gas prices had increased by a doller per gallon. But when I found myself complaining, I remembered that "I'm too blessed to be stressed."

From overdraft to overflow, I used to depend on my airline benefits to travel standby. Now, I never have to drive or fly on a "shoestring" budget. With multiple bank accounts and the discipline to save my money and not give it all away, no longer do I keep a negative balance, or accumulated, overdraft fees. Just as I could never afford a simple car wash and was forced to drive dirty, I now have a monthly membership where I can get as many washes as I could have ever imagined. Embarrassed by three repossessions, not only is my SUV paid in full, I was told that my credit is good enough for me to lease a new, luxury car whenever I'm ready.

Sometimes God will allow you to go through the worse to appreciate His best. But even when I did not have a ride at all, He gave me "ride-or-try" friends." But look what happens before I could complete this 2nd edition. I received an email from Discover Card with this message: "Congratulations! We've noticed your excellent credit management overall and increased your credit line to **$7,000.**" Hands down, this was my greatest reward/increase in the history of my credit! ***"This is the LORD'S doing; it is marvelous in [my] eyes"*** (Psa. 118:23 KJV with emphasis added). Finally, God has destroyed the yoke and rebuked the devour!

I may not have the big house, **or** the luxury car **(yet)**; but for now, my Toyota is low maintenance with better gas mileage (the power of essentialism). When I have gotten my oil change in the past two years, there has never been a need for them to sell me on anything extra. I already feel like I have everything because for once, there is no lack, shortage, or insufficiency. Not only has my soul been restored, this must be what it feels like to lie down in green pastures, beside the still waters (Psa. 23:2-3). ***"He has made everything beautiful and appropriate in its time"*** (Eccl. 3:11 AMP). To you, this testimony of favor may not indicate wealth or riches, or even success, but these are the blessings and benefits that make me content in the state I'm in.

From overdraft to overflow, Psalm 66:12 KJV (with emphasis added) is my new reality. ***"Thou hast caused men to ride over our heads; we went through fire and through water: but Thou broughtest us*** [ME] ***out into a wealthy place."*** I am so thankful that God did this, so that now, ALL the credit goes to HIM! "It 'ain't' over until it's GOOD!" Why can I say this with confidence? Now that it's good, IT'S OVER! Another good reason why I didn't get married, I had to wait on *purpose*, **and** until **ALL** these things worked out for my good (Rom. 8:28). Everyone in the Bible that Jesus touched got healed. But the woman with the issue touched Him, and she was made whole. When He has to come and touch you, you will get a miracle, but when you pursue Him, you get it ALL.

In my opinion, God allowed the Israelites to wander around in the wilderness for 40 years to reveal to them what was in their own hearts. In 1980, I shook the preacher's hand that opened a door to making the biggest pact with the enemy. After being in bondage for 15 years, it took another 25 years to be released from the curse. Exactly 40 years later, I am finally on the other side of my wilderness experience. We must learn who we are before we can show others what God always knew. So never limit a person to who they really are, by where they were before they came out. And you (reader), never be limited by your own limitations. The very thing that made life horrible is the very thing from your past that will push you forward.

While the BIG comeback is greater than the original setback, the framework is likened to resurrecting the buried-self. The stages of this model included: reappearing of the buried-self, resuscitating the buried self, renovating the buried-self, regenerating the buried-self, reanimating the buried-self, and reincarnating the buried-self. #NEWYEAR-NEWME! Believe it or not, some folks can't even die until they see me live. In fact, a great observation is that God allowed them to come into my life to kill the old me so that He could resurrect the new me. So thank you.

Married or single, can't nothing stop a cycle like a seed. Sometimes, it's not a bad thing to look back and dig up what the devil thought he buried. He buried me, but what he didn't realize is that I was a seed. That's why you must be careful who you leave for dead. When you return to this empty tomb, you will see that my dead situation has changed to Psalm 23:5 (KJV): ***"Thou preparest a table before me in the presence of mine enemies: Thou anointest my head with oil; my cup runneth over."***

On October 16, 2020, I had a dream of being robbed. The robber got away and came back the 2nd time. This time, the "deceased" man looked at me with frustration and just threw my wallet on the ground. In amazement, I said: "I got all my money back." Ultimately, I was able to go back and pick up money and things that were lost in the first robbery. In this moment, I remember feeling how special I was to God, and how He is **in** love with me. I recall thinking that, not only is Satan being FORCED to give back what he took; I am recovering ALL.

Then, I was reminded of 2 Chronicles 20:25 (NAS): ***"When Jehoshaphat and his people came to take the spoil, they found much among them, including goods, garments and valuable things which they took for themselves, more than they could carry. And they were three days taking the spoil because there was so much."*** After the dream but before I could wake up good, Mama Delores sent me a random Cash App for $50, and said: "Lunch on me." This was not my norm, okay. But the 50 was prophetic of my Jubilee season. *From overdraft to overflow,* I am about to be in a place where I have plenty of days with special deliveries.

Finally, here is what has been the game-changer for me. I made the decision to never compromise the essence of my story; yet, I must not base my existence off my scars. The scars are a part of my story, but I cannot play the victim's role by blaming others for circumstances that were created by my own decision. Actually, the only time that I dwell on the past is when I am giving language to a fiery that interrupts a pattern. And the only reason that a person may be bothered by my story is that they chose to read it. Wherefore, it's Karen's story; Karen's book, and Karen's way. If you did not get relief as a result of my release, the message was not for you. Either way, I spoke my peace and set my "own-az" free. And oh, by the way, in the event that you were offended by my use of the zinger, "az," I trust that you have learned by now that it was used as a person's title and not a person's ass. "Okay?"

Putting it mildly, I have had to burst some spiritual blisters and remove some "bunions," in order to walk in total forgiveness. Thus, a word to the wise: since fear and faith are creative forces, avoid negative people, caustic words, and disparaging thoughts. They all create the wrong energy. In broken English, a Chinese tattoo artist once said of a tattoo that read, "Born to win:" "Before tattoo on body, tattoo on mind: 'Uma-sho-dem'." So use your energy to show them what-you-working-with. And let this be your prayer: "Father-God, since I'm working with You, I just want to take this time to thank You for loving me like a father should love his child, like a good shepherd should care for his sheep, and like a man who is in sacred covenant with his wife."

THE PROPHETIC PIVOT

Now in the midst of a world-wide pandemic, this is the season (whether married or single) that you will discover how strong your faith is and how real your God is. A perfect time to make the *prophetic pivot,* the only way to be empowered by what you were limited by is to make sure that your anchor is secure. Consequently, there will never be business as usual. And since God has changed the whole trajectory of traditional church, people are becoming more and more content with cyber church.

One of the most powerful posts that I have seen on Facebook during this season, Michael Payton speaks my sentiments. He wrote: "I have my national license, clergy collar, Jurisdictional I.D., Elder's ring, and Cross in a Ziploc bag. But if Church stays the same after this, focused primarily on reports and meetings, disgusting banquets and dinners (planned only to raise money), protocol and performance, platinum and platforms, rather than ministry, outreach, education and servant-hood, we have learned NOTHING."

In echoing Dr. Kynan Bridges, I recently heard him say during a Facebook Live that God is destroying the archetypes that we have been attached to, that were really never Him. I agree that crisis and casual Christianity is over. As a matter of fact, our old way of doing things is over! Interestingly so, Dr. Bridges concept of accepting the "Mark of the Beast" is embracing the world system into our minds. That includes the ideologies of this world, the doctrine of devils, the diabolical world of manipulation and control, intimidation, anti-God, anti-Christ, anti-religion, anti-family, anti-marriage, etc.

Whereas many Christians have already accepted this concept of the Mark of the Beast, the premise is that the enemy has instituted a new world order into your mind. At the same time, God is creating His new world (read the 1st Chapter of Hebrews). Guess what! God's new world is **OUTSIDE** of the four walls of a church building, which has become **man's** world and a comfort zone that made him feel empowered, entitled and in control. Now we must learn and be willing to share ministry OUTSIDE THE BOX!

If you are to remain relevant and become fit for the future, you must operate like a futurist and realize that the church has been caught up in the "clouds." Along these lines, I agree with Larry D. Reid that the church has left the building. As I am fully awaken to the fact that Jesus taught/trained in the synagogue, He reached and preached in the streets. At the level of this revelation, the church has never been a building; the body of Christ **made** it to be about a building. Think about it: unless it was attached by grant money, most churches did not start doing outreach until the pandemic hit. Why? The building has made it too comfortable for us to fulfill the mission of Luke 14:23. That validates my point: the church is an assembly, and **where**ver we assemble together, be it in the building or in the "clouds," we are still fulfilling the Scripture, Hebrews 3:13. God is not coming back after a building; He's coming back after a church (a people)!

Consistent with Dr. Bridges, God's new world is the Kingdom of God and HIS righteousness, and in a space where the peace and the joy of the Holy Spirit is our daily portion. It's the time and place where we are getting ready to **release** the Kingdom and operate **in** the Kingdom wherever we are and wherever we go. Indeed, God is getting ready to do a new thing, and I would be remiss to close this book without allowing you to become a part of this *prophetic pivot.*

To say the least, Covid-19 is definitely not the sinners' "market." In this new season of **CHANGE**, "if you are hanging on by a thread, make sure that it's the hem of Jesus garment" (r/TrueChristian). To experience this Christ as your Lord and Savior, consider this book as my pulpit and wherever you are, as your altar. Since salvation is as easy as ABC, **Admit** that you are a sinner (Rom. 5:12). **Believe** in your heart that Christ died for your sins (John 3:16), and that He was raised from the dead. Then, **Confess** with your mouth that HE is Lord (Rom. 10:9). ***"Yet to all who did receive Him, to those who believed in His name, He gave the right to become children of God"*** (John 1:12 NIV). Also read Colossians 1:22-23.

The same as He has made me, you are now ready for my Master to make you His "Master's-piece." Welcome to the family of God! Even though Marcus Rogers prediction/prophecy of Trump's win was totally-off, I must agree with him on this: "When the little girl is healed, the woman will show up. And when a man finds out who he is in Christ, he finds out what kind of woman he needs in his life." Now, make the 'pivot,' and "go get 'yo' blessing!"

REFERENCES

WHY DIDN'T I GET MARRIED?
EITHER BOAZ OR "NO-AZ," I'M WAITING ON **PURPOSE**

Cover Design & Dr. Reid's Custom-made T-shirt Design by Arthur Purdue: https://www.facebook.com/arthur.purdue.18

Photo Credits by Pixabay.com

Fenton, F. & Jones, S. E. (2013). Moses' eighth speech, Part 1, law of divorce. Retrieved from https:www.gods-kingdom-ministries.net/daily-webblogs/2013/05-2013/moses-eighth-speech-post-1-law-of-divorce/

Jakes, T. D. (2016). Crazy choices. Dallas, TX: T.D. Jakes Ministries.

Jakes, T. D. (2016). Is it well with your soul? Dallas, TX: T. D. Jakes Ministries.

McKeown, G. (2014). *Essentialism: The disciplined pursuit of less.* New York, NY: Crown Publishing Group.

Parnitzke Smith, C., & Freyd, J. J. (2013). Dangerous safe havens: Institutional betrayal exacerbates sexual trauma. *Journal of Traumatic Stress, 26*(1), 119-124. doi: 10.1002/jts.21778

Reid, K. D. (2017). "Hey 'Adam,' 'where you at'?" Minneapolis, MN: AuthorHouse.

Reid, K. D. (2014). *God, why didn't he cover me?* Undressed by man, but addressed by God. Minneapolis, MN: AuthorHouse.

Reid, K. D. (2010). *From man's abuse to the woman God loosed.* Minneapolis, MN:AuthorHouse.

Rutter, P. (1997). *Sex in the forbidden zone: When therapists, doctors, clergy, teachers and other men in power betray women's trust.* New York, NY: Random House.

Smith, L. (n.d.). Broken but not beyond repair. Miami, FL: Hope of Refuge Ministries

Sommers-Flanagan, R. S., & Sommers-Flanagan, J. S. (2007). *Becoming an ethical and helping professional.* Hoboken, NJ: John Wiley & Sons, Inc.

Stockstill, L. (2014). Restoring integrity in the pulpit. Retrieved from http://ministrytodaymag.com/index.php/ministry-leadership/ethics/20596 restoring integrity-in-the-pulpit

Tenney, T. (1998). *The God chasers.* Shippensburg, PA:Destiny Image, Inc.

ABOUT THE AUTHOR

With over 10 years of hands-on experience in church Administration, Dr. Reid earned a Bachelor of Science Degree in Education from the University of Memphis (formerly known as Memphis State University), and a Master of Arts Degree in Management and Leadership from Webster University. Upon earning a 2nd Masters degree in Human Services at Capella University where she maintained a 4.0 GPA as a doctoral candidate, her passion to equip the saints for the work of ministry led her to complete her doctoral program in Christian Organizational Leadership at the Newburgh Theological Seminary in Indiana.

Dr. Reid is the President/CEO of The Twin Ministries Empowerment Network, Inc., a 501c3 non-profit organization, whose brand signifies "two ministries coming together with one vision to empower the community and promote excellence in leadership." God-employed as a full-time author and ministry-gift to the Body of Christ, Dr. Reid was an 11-year employee of Pinnacle Airlines (a wholly-owned subsidiary of Delta Airlines), where she was the recipient of the 1st Annual, Recognition Award – Employee of the Year, for her professionalism in Customer Service.

Having found her forte as a committed author and entrepreneur, she currently serves as an Editorial Specialist and Leadership Development Consultant. From an abuse victim to a breast cancer and lupus survivor, Dr. Karen D. Reid is also a **W**oman of **W**ord, **W**isdom, **W**orship & **W**ealth. W.O.W.W.W.W.! Realistically so, she has ultimately become "more than a conqueror," and the sum total of a working project in progress – life after death. Thus, her personal tagline: "When you evolve into **who** you really **are**, you won't mind embracing **why** you **were**." #K.DR

OTHER BOOKS & RESOURCES BY DR. REID:

TRILOGY: PART ONE
GOD, WHY DIDN'T HE COVER ME?
UNDRESSED BY MAN BUT ADDRESSED BY GOD

TRILOGY: PART TWO
FROM MAN'S ABUSE TO THE WOMAN GOD LOOSED
PAIN, POISON – PURPOSE

TRILOGY: PART THREE
HE GOT ME PREGNANT ON PURPOSE
FROM MISTRESS TO MINISTRY

"HEY 'ADAM', 'WHERE YOU AT'?"
TAKE A STAND AND BE THE MAN

INTERVENTIONS TO ADDRESS VICTIMS
OF CLERGY SEXUAL MISCONDUCT

COMPREHESIVE ADMINISTRATIVE TRAINING
MANUAL FOR 21ST-CENTURY MINISTRY LEADERS
(Includes 50 Servant Job Descriptions for Servant Leaders)

LEADERSHIP DEVELOPMENT TRAINING 101
SOLUTION-ORIENTED DEVELOPMENT
COURSES FOR LEADERS & STAFF
(PART TWO IS FORTHCOMING)

THE REFERENCE & TEACHING MANUALS
FOR WOMEN IN MINISTRY
(PARTS ONE & TWO)

GODLY LIVES MATTER
(A REFERENCE & TEACHING MANUAL
FOR MEN'S MINISTRY)

2020 VISION
ADMINISTRATION & LEADERSHIP APPLICATIONS
FOR EVOLVING MINISTRIES

**EVERYTHING ELSE YOU NEED TO KNOW
ABOUT CHURCH & MINISTRY
THE COMPLIANCE SIDE OF MINISTRY: VOLUMES 1-3**
COMPLIMENTARY FOR **GOLDSTAR**
SPONSORS ONLY/Sponsorship Packages

BONUS OFFER: If you are an aspiring
author and would like to receive my
COACHING TIPS for 1st -TIME AUTHORS,
inquire at: www.karenreid.org

**ALSO DR. REID'S CUSTOM-DESIGNED T-SHIRT APPAREL
"BREAST CANCER CONQUEROR" (NAHUM 1:9)**

**(BLACK T-SHIRT WITH PINK ACCENT COLOR,
WITH NAHUM 1:9 ON THE BACK)**

YOUR SUPPORT SPEAKS VOLUMES!

For the latest information and up-to-date
editions of K.DR's inspirational books,
PLEASE PLACE YOUR ORDERS AT:
AuthorHouse.com
888-519-5121
or www.karenreid.org

For the latest information and up-to-date editions of the
Training/Leadership Manuals & T.T.M.'S Reference Books,
PLEASE PLACE YOUR ORDERS AT:
or www.karenreid.org
or (901) 236-3946

Please email me your "take-away" from this reading experience: www.thetwinministries@yahoo.com

FACEBOOK:
Karen D. Reid: https://www.facebook.com/karen.d.reid.1
The Twin Ministries@DrKarenDReid: https://www.facebook.com/DrKarenDReid/

Mailing Address:
PO Box 752613
Memphis, TN 38175

FOR TAX-DEDUCTIBLE DONATIONS
CASH APP: $KReid17
ZELLE: (901) 634-2667 or thetwinministries@yahoo.com
PAYPAL: thetwinministries@yahoo.com0

Printed in the United States
by Baker & Taylor Publisher Services